Mo...

a Pearl Lake Novel

Book 3

Aquila Thorne

Moonlit Road
A Pearl Lake Novel
Book 3 of Pearl Lake the Series
Copyright © 2021 Aquila Thorne
ISBN: 9798413281765
Previously published by me, Tina Marie

Books in the series

---

1. https://books2read.com/AQBenandAbbi

2. https://books2read.com/AQMoonlit-Night

3. https://books2read.com/AQMoonlitRoad

4. https://books2read.com/ATHeavenintheMoonlight

5. https://books2read.com/AQInnAtPearlLake

6. https://books2read.com/ATlanesdestiny

7. https://books2read.com/AQTimsbar-

8. https://books2read.com/AQ-herChristmaswish

Dear Readers

Just in a case you're joining me now, I wanted to mention a few things. The series is best read in order, although the books can be read individually, some readers might get confused. Also, I've combined the first two books of the series into one, Moonlit Night. A couple of reasons why I did that are:

1. Money is tight for a lot of people. Don't get me wrong, I need it just as much as the next person, but I too know what it's like to want to escape from the realities of life within a good book and not always have the extra money to do so.

2. The title of the second book I think might have scared a few readers off, something that was never intended. As a new writer, when I wrote these books, I never wrote them like many authors do. I didn't plot or write to reader expectation or to market.

I just simply wrote them. The characters had a mind of their own and took me on a journey as well. One that I had fun writing and one that allowed me to escape the realities of life. Something that I wish for all my readers. My books will always have relatable characters and that comedy factor with a little suspense and of course romance.

A few times I've been told to there are typos in my books. I want to mention that I am Canadian and as a Canadian; I write in British English. There may be a time or two that you happen along a word that is spelled with American English and the reason for that is I've lived all my life close to the Canadian/US border. Because of that, sometimes I switch back and forth, an example would be that I use imperial instead of metric when describing feet instead of meters and miles instead of kilometers. Other words, you might think are typos if you're living in the US would be any word that ends in 'OR', like color, honor, favor, flavor, neighbor, all those words and more, over here in Canada have a 'U' added, colour, honour, favour, flavour, neighbour and so on. Also, words ending with 'ER', theater, center, once again, here in Canada we spell them theatre, centre, etc. With that said and keeping it in mind, I welcome you to Moonlit Road, I do hope you enjoy it!

Prologue

Abbi sat in front of her computer, just finishing up her last chapter.

Finally! She thought as she typed the last word. She sat back staring at the screen, thinking how only six months ago she had been struggling with every word she typed. Odd how life turns out.

Brutus' loud yawn had her glancing at him as he laid in the sun, Molly and Lucy were at his side. She got up, walking to the control panel for the wall of windows. She opened one, allowing the crisp air outside to come in. She marveled at the view of the lake they provided. It was a picture-perfect day, blue skies, brilliant sunshine, the fall colours were spectacular this year. She couldn't wait until it snowed. She could see it already in her mind. The lake frozen, the sun sparkling off the snow-covered pine trees. Ben had been right. This was the perfect room for her to write in.

They had used his bedroom until they had completed the addition. Ben got the bathroom he wanted. He claimed it was for Abbi, but she secretly knew different. And she got the bedroom of her dreams. Not that she hadn't already had that, but this one was for them both this time. She smiled. How excited he was designing it all himself, with her input of course.

She moved into his home the week after her party. She frowned, thinking back to the BBQ... not realizing at the time, how close Ben had come to being shot. Thank God, Steve saw Raven's intentions. Otherwise, she very well could have lost him that day. The thought drove her nearly to the edge of insanity. If Raven had succeeded, she'd be the one sitting in a jail cell now. As it was, Raven's case was before the courts. The Crown Attorney was pushing for life. She just hoped to God, he got it, for all he had done... especially to Ben.

Oh, how she missed him! He'd been away for a month and a half now. He and Mark had been off shooting another movie. This time a comedy, both having a main role in it. That was another thing... Mark had convinced Abbi to let him rent her house. He told her he had two willing roommates to move in with him as well. So, it would never stand empty as this one had.

Ava and Kim both shocked the hell out of her when they announced they were staying in Pearl Lake. Ava had sold her spa in Windsor and opened a new one on the edge of the village in a gorgeous Victorian home. And Kim, she was helping Doc Spence at the clinic. Her reason for staying was she couldn't bring herself to leave her partners in crime. Abbi chuckled at the thought of what those three had gotten up to in the past few months.

Sighing, she looked at her watch. Just a few more hours... Ben would stroll through the door and take her in his arms. A thrill went through her body at the thought of it. Their flight took off eight hours ago from somewhere in South America. She had such an uneasy feeling whenever he was flying. He always reassured her that nothing would go wrong, but it didn't help any.

Hmm, I should know what country they are coming from. She'd just turned to look at the itinerary of their trip sitting on her desk, when she heard a car flying into the driveway. Ben, he must be home earlier than he thought! She rushed to the window, frowning as she saw Ava's car come to a sliding halt.

That's odd... Turning from the window, she crossed the room at a hurried pace. She all but ran the length of the walkway to the stairs, her foot touching the bottom step just as the front door flew open.

Ava stood there panting for a moment, her face pale.

"Ava? Honey, are you sick? What's wrong?" Abbi felt sick herself at that very moment.

Shaking her head, Ava sucked in a deep breath and said, "I tried to get here as fast as I could. Why didn't you answer your phone?"

"I was writing. I have it on silent? What's going on?"

Ava waved her hand. "It's all over the news. Turn on the TV," she said. Hurrying into the living room Abbi grabbed the remote, stabbing the power button on.

There before them on the screen was a live viewing of a plane wreckage. With a sinking feeling, Abbi sat down on the arm of the couch. "Ava... what are you trying to tell me..." Abbi knew exactly what she was trying to tell her. Her brain, however, needed to hear it, as her heart was in denial.

Ava turned to her mother, her tears streaming down her face.

"Mom," she went to her then. "Ben and Mark's plane went down twenty minutes after takeoff."

"BEN?" MARK SWALLOWED hard. His throat felt like he hadn't had a drink of anything in a week. "Buddy... can you hear me?"

He lay still on the ground. Straining to hear anything. Only silence met his ears. Slowly moving, he tested each limb to see if anything was broken. His left wrist was the only thing that hurt like a bitch.

A loud screech broke through the silence causing him to jerk straight up. He sat, gazing around at his surroundings for any signs of life.

Where the hell is Ben? And why am I sitting on the ground in the middle of a forest?

He remembered now. They were on their way back to Canada when the plane started to shake and shudder.

Mark glanced to his left, seeing Ben with his cellphone in his hand. He looked at him, both knowing the peril they were in, knowing this could be the end. "I had to send Abbi a text to tell her one last time that I love her."

Mark scoffed at him, trying to reassure him that they would get through this... despite him having doubts to the contrary. "Man, everything will be fine. We will be back home in no time. And you can ask her to marry you like you planned." Mark put an arm around Ben then, both men hugging.

They felt the plane rapidly falling to earth. The air masks dropped, both grabbed for them, putting them on. Being frequent flyers, they knew the drill, as they ducked and tucked their heads between their legs. A sound of metal ripping and roaring wind was the only sign that it had damaged the plane as it grazed the treetops. Their section landed with a sickening crash of metal on branches.

The next thing Mark remembered was calling out to Ben. Panic started to set in with the realization that he might be the only survivor until he heard a faint groan.

Mark stood up looking around. Luggage, metal, trees, and bodies were strewn about him. He caught movement out of the corner of his eye. Rushing over he saw a woman still strapped in her seat. "Miss, are you okay?" Mark asked, concerned when he saw the gash on her brow, blood pooling into her eye. Looking around for something clean, he tore open the nearest suitcase. Grabbing a t-shirt, he ripped it into a makeshift bandage wrapping it around her head.

He unbuckled her from her seat and laid her on the ground, telling her to lay still.

He went to the next victim. Finding the man to be fine except for a few bumps and bruises, he learned his name was Hank. Together they started helping others.

After a while, Mark still hadn't come across Ben. He saw there was one more person needing help... and they weren't moving. He made his way over to them, seeing that they were wearing the same colour of jeans Ben had on. Mark had to stop for a minute, steeling himself for what he may find. He slowly went to the person. It relieved him to see that it wasn't Ben, but instantly he was filled with sadness. The person hadn't made it.

Mark hurried back to the others. "Hey, Hank. Did you come across a man, brown hair, about yay high? Speaks with a British accent?"

"No, sorry, I didn't..." Hank replied, earnestly.

"Thanks, man." Mark turned away, glancing around, in case he missed someone laying there. He stood with his hands on his hips. Worriedly, he muttered aloud, "Ben... Where the hell are you, buddy?"

ABBI DIDN'T HEAR AVA. She focused her eyes and ears on the reporter's sober tone: "The cast and crew of Stoned River's plane crashed shortly after takeoff."

Photos of the plane were now on the screen as the reporter continued. "It's confirmed that cast members Ben Quinn and Mark Donovan were to be on this flight that was en route to Toronto Canada."

Their photos were now on the screen. Abbi got up and walked to the TV. She laid her hand on Ben's photo, the tears now falling from her eyes.

"There have been some casualties, but at this time we aren't sure if they are among those who perished in this tragic accident."

Abbi put her hand down. She stood there looking at the TV.

Wouldn't I feel it if he were gone?

She didn't believe it. She refused to believe it after everything they had gone through... she would know.

"Mom?" Ava sniffled, putting a hand on Abbi's arm. "Are you okay?"

Abbi turned, looking at her. "Yes honey, I'm fine." Taking a steadying breath, Abbi knew what she had to do. "Ava, go pack a bag."

Ava gaped at her. Oh my God, she's lost it. Shaking her head in confusion, she said, "What?"

"I said... go pack a bag. We are going to that plane wreck. I'll call Kim. Both of you better be ready in a half-hour, or I'm leaving without you," she said, pulling out her phone.

She hated flying. Ben knew that. When he needed to go back to Madrid to finish up his scenes for The Jasper Killings, true to her promise, she begrudgingly went with him... Tears formed in her eyes as her mind replayed the beautiful memories that they made there.

She, of course, was drunk as a skunk on the flights there and back. Thank goodness he was there to take care of her. Otherwise, she'd never have returned to Canada.

She chewed her bottom lip, waiting for Kim to pick up. "Hi, Kim..."

"Hey, Abbi, did you hear..."

Abbi cut her off. They didn't have time for that. "Yes, I heard. Ava came by and told me. Can you ask Doc to stop by and check on the dogs for me? Better yet, ask him to stay here for a while? I have no idea how long we will be." She paused listening to the exchange in the background.

"Uh, Abbi... he wants to know... who is we?"

"Tell him, we as in you, Ava and me. We are going down there to find them."

"She told me to tell you that 'we' is me, Ava and her and... wait... what?" Kim yelled into the phone.

"Be ready in ten minutes. Ava is packing for you, as we speak." She hung up with Kim still jabbering.

She looked through her contact list. Stabbing the digits, she waited for it to connect.

"Nigel. Abbi Peterson here. I need you to find me a plane..." She listened... "No, not a rental. One for sale.... How soon? Oh, in about an hour I'll be in Toronto, can you make it happen? Great, and make sure a pilot goes with it... a very experienced one, please. Right! I'll get Ava to transfer the money on the way down. Thanks, Nigel" She hung up the phone.

Sending a prayer to the powers that be she swallowed hard at what she was about to undertake. Speaking aloud she said, "Ben..." She had to pause. The lump in her throat caused her voice to crack as the tears streamed down her face. She had to continue, maybe just maybe he would hear her voice. Heaving a shaky sigh, she cleared her throat. "I'm on my way. Please, babe be safe. I know you're out there, somewhere... you have to be."

She grabbed her keys, kissed each animal on the head, telling them to be good, and headed out the door. She knew she was crazy for doing this, but she'd be crazy not to. She refused to give up on the one man who had changed her life so completely... one who loved her with his very soul. Ben had once promised her he'd follow her to the ends of the earth. She just never told him that she'd do the same for him.

Chapter 1

They were travelling along the highway at a pace any Indie race car driver would be proud of when Kim couldn't take it anymore. Gripping the headrest of the passenger seat where Ava her niece was sitting, Kim yelled, "Abbi, slow the hell down! You know, I can see the speedo and 160 km/h is not the speed limit. In fact, it's stunt driving." She shook her head knowing it was a waste of her breath; her sister was on a mission.

Abbi was zoned out. And just like the last time Kim went on a tirade, she ignored her sister. Zipping past the cars and transports, her only thought was that she needed to get to Ben, and now. The plan had been to fly. Nigel, her real estate agent had 'connections' and assured her that he could find her a jet; and he did, but not for at least a week. God Himself couldn't keep her waiting for a week. They had to leave now, and their only choice was to drive. She hated travelling on the 401, as much as she hated flying. But nothing was going to stop her, not even her fear. She gripped the steering wheel a little tighter as she read the sign on the side of the road... London, population 353,000, 4 inter-changes.

Great. Just what I need. Traffic is going to pick up again...

"Mom?" Ava's soft voice broke into her musings.

"Yeah?" Abbi responded, glancing down at the speedometer. Horrified at how fast she was going, she eased her foot off the gas pedal.

Ava knew that look on her mother's face and it wasn't good. They had been on the road for 5 hours. Traffic had been brutal through Toronto. But that hadn't stopped her mother from keeping the speed at a minimum of a 130 km/h. She had to be getting tired. "Why don't we stop for a minute? There is a service station just past London. We can grab a bite to eat and a coffee."

Kim chimed in, groaning. "Yeah, and I really need to take a piss."

Abbi adjusted the rear-view mirror until she caught Kim's image in the reflection. She *was* squirming an awful lot. She nodded. "Fine. Five minutes and we're back on the road." She hated the thought of even stopping that long. But she had to admit she needed to make a stop to the ladies' room herself.

It was starting to get dark, with the city lights of London behind them Abbi stepped on the gas pedal. The sooner they got there, the sooner they could leave. Ava and Kim grabbed the 'oh shit' bars as the SUV swerved around a transport and flew past it. Not one of them saw the OPP cruiser in front of it until it was too late.

"Son of a bitch!" Abbi swore, as the cruiser's lights engaged.

The signs for the service station were right there; just 5 more kilometers. She had to stop. And she would, at the service station. Never batting an eye, Abbi kept her speed steady. Mentally she counted down each kilometer.

Kim felt like she was watching a tennis match. Her head bobbed back and forth between the cop in the rear window and her sister at the wheel. She about peed her pants when she saw another police car on the other side of the highway, fast approaching. It made a U-turn in the emergency lane and joined in the pursuit.

With lights and sirens blaring, Kim screeched, "Umm... *Abbi? You gonna stop before they send some more?!*"

"Mom? Pull over before you get yourself arrested!"

Not trusting her sister to stop, Kim leaned between the seats and pointed, "There's the merge lane for the service station. Get the hell over Abbi."

Abbi quickly clicked on her turn signal. Slowing down, she exited the highway and came to a stop in an open area of the parking lot.

"Jesus, Abbi what the hell were you thinking?" Kim asked, shaking her head.

With a heavy sigh, Abbi rummaged in the center console for her ownership and insurance.

"I'm not... thinking that is." She shot a quick glance to her two companions. "If I don't get arrested. One of you will need to drive. I um... I need a break," she whispered, her voice cracking at her admission.

"Sure." Kim's voice softened. "One of us will drive, won't we Ava?"

"Yeah mom, we can take turns." Ava reached over and gave her mom a hug.

A knock at Abbi's window had them all jumping. Turning to look out the glass, Abbi saw the police officer standing there.

She hit the power window button. As it lowered, she glanced up at the angry face peering down at her.

"Ma'am, just what the hell were you thinking? I need your license and registration, please."

Without a word, Abbi handed over the requested documents.

"You do realize you were going 160, right? I could haul you in for stunt driving and impound your car. Mind telling me what's so important that you're willing to risk the lives of others on the road and your passengers?" The officer bent down to look at Ava and Kim.

"Ah..." Abbi started to speak than shut her mouth.

"Well, helloo Officer." Kim could clearly see how attractive the cop was. "You see, she's not in her right state of mind at the moment," she supplied. Pointing to her head, she spun her finger in circles, silently conveying that Abbi was off her rocker. For good measure, she softly muttered "cuckoo", as she turned to look out her window.

The cop looked taken aback. "Is that so?" he asked, searching Abbi's face.

Ava leaned across Abbi just then.

"What she means is, my mother... err... Abbi here," she jerked her head towards her. "Has had quite a shock. You see, there was a plane crash..."

Frowning, he looked between Ava and Kim. The doubtful look on his face had Ava clamping her mouth shut. She didn't want to say anything more in case the officer decided to haul them all off to jail.

"Then why is she driving, and not one of you?" he asked sourly as the other officer approached with his hand on his gun.

"She didn't ask?" Kim said, thinking he was insane for even suggesting it. One didn't tell Abbi what to do when she was in this state of mind. She would bite their heads off if they did.

Abbi felt like a child at that moment. She had to say something, to fess up to her crime of speeding like a lunatic down the busiest highway in North America.

"Whoa, wait, hold up." Abbi held her hand up for some calm. She didn't feel very calm now, but she had to take control. "Officer. Wait, what is your name, again?" she asked scrunching her brow in thought. She was sure he'd mentioned it.

"I didn't say... Miss..." He pulled out a penlight and flashed the beam across her license.

Abbi was suddenly blinded by that same beam when it was directed at her, and she squinted from the onslaught.

"Abbi? Abbi Petersen, aka Abbi Stevens?" Tim turned to the other officer and said, "I know them Bill, it's fine."

"Ahh... yes? What do you mean 'I know them'?" Abbi asked, holding her hand up as she tried to shield her eyes. "Do I know *you* or something?" She blinked rapidly as her eyes started to water. "Could you please get that light out of my face?"

"Oh, shit. Sorry. It's Tim. Tim Steel? We went to high school together." He grinned when the recognition hit Abbi's face.

With a squeal, Abbi grabbed the door handle, shoved it open, and unsuccessfully launched herself at Tim. Her seat belt halting her actions, slammed her back against the seat.

"Some things never change, do they Abbi?" Tim chuckled. "Here, let me give you a hand."

He leaned in, reached over her, and unbuckled the seat belt. Taking her hand, he guided her out of the vehicle and into his arms.

Ava and Kim's eyes bugged as they cried out in unison. "*Whaaaat?!*" Unsure of what to do they sat, gaping at the two hugging.

Ava was the first to break the silence, grabbing hold of her aunt's arm, she shook it. "Uh...Aunt Kim... are you seeing what I'm seeing?"

Kim just stared with her mouth agape.

Ava snapped her eyes to look at Kim. "Did you know about this and not tell me?" she hissed, before turning back to look at her mother embracing the stranger.

"How the hell would *I* know? They... they do seem to know each other. If you catch my drift," Kim stammered.

"Yeah. What do you think we should do?" Fearing she would miss something. Ava risked another glance at Kim.

"I don't know." Yanking on her door handle, Kim said, "Let's go, we need to intervene."

"Wait for me!" Ava scrambled out her door, rounded the front of the SUV, and abruptly plowed into Kim's back.

"Jesus, Mary and Joseph," Kim muttered under her breath. There, before them stood Abbi and the officer, Tim, talking in hushed tones. He was rubbing Abbi's back as she cried on his shoulder.

"No, no, no! This is not a good thing," Ava whispered. While she watched she shook her head back and forth then gave Kim a shove from behind. "Stop them!"

"*Me*? Why me? She's *your* mother."

"You've known her longer. Besides, she's used to you butting in."

"Fine... but you're coming with me."

Together, they slinked as one, stopping within two feet of the duo. Kim shifted from one foot to the other, took a deep breath and said, "Ahem. Abbi. We need to finish up here if you want to get to Ben." Kim scooted closer with Ava clinging to her backside, talking in a soothing tone as she did. "You remember Ben... don't you?"

Abbi swallowed hard; her eyes red from crying, she backed away from Tim and wiped her tears off his jacket. She nodded, not trusting herself to speak just yet.

Kim had never seen Abbi so upset before in her life, she didn't know if it was because of Ben or from seeing Tim in her life again. Seeing how this was the first time Kim had the privilege of laying her eyes on the officer, she wasn't entirely sure what Tim meant to Abbi. One thing she was certain of, that it had to end here and now.

Tim caught the emphasis on Ben's name. "Kim, is it?"

At her nod he continued. "Abbi was just telling me about Ben. I can understand why you guys are in a rush, which is why I offered to escort you to Windsor, but I can only go as far as the Ambassador Bridge." Tim looked at Ava than Kim. "But it's only on one condition."

Both had that 'caught in headlights on the side of a darkened road' look, just like a deer.

Finally, Abbi broke her silence and said, "Tim doesn't want me driving."

At the same time, Kim, and Ava, said, "Of course not!" Relief clearly on their faces, they rushed over to hug Abbi and pulled her a safe distance from Tim.

"Then it's settled. I'll just radio into dispatch; explain the situation while you all go do your business in there." Tim pointed to the service station.

Kim snickered. "I was afraid I'd have to get physical with you Tim, err... Officer Tim. I'll just shut up now." *I really needed to learn to keep my mouth shut*, she thought, as she felt the blush rise to her cheeks. "Well, you know... Abbi and Ben..." she tried to smooth her outburst over.

"I do, and Abbi and I have always just been friends. Right, Abbs?"

Abbi smiled and nodded. She still didn't trust herself to speak too much. And, felt like she was on the edge of a meltdown. That wouldn't do. She had to find Ben. Even if it meant identifyi— *No! Do NOT go there, Abbi!! He is alive...*

Ava put an arm around her mother. "Come on, Mom, let's get something to eat." She guided her towards the building while Kim followed, staring at the police officer with a dreamy look in her eyes.

Abbi sat with her head in her hands at a booth, waiting for Ava and Kim to return with their food. She laid her purse on the table and planted her face on it. She didn't care that people were shooting strange looks her way. She was so unbelievably spent. If she had the strength, she might have just shot them back a look or two... or given them the one-finger salute. She regretted the thought the second it entered her mind. Shooting the middle finger was not something she would do.

She was about to push herself up when her purse started to vibrate against her face. *What the...?* She sat up and started rummaging through it to find the culprit. Her phone... She never had it on vibrate. Ava. She must have turned it on after the reporters started to call. Tapping the screen, she saw there were a couple of texts and 10 missed calls. She scrolled through the call log.

Thank you, God... It was Mark. With shaking hands, Abbi quickly stabbed his number. He picked up after the second ring.

"Mark. Hi, it's Abbi, is Ben with you?" She closed her eyes, waiting.

"Hey, Abbi. Uh, how's it going?" He sounded so... distraught. "Mark... where are you? Is Ben with you?"

"I guess you heard about the plane crash, huh?"

Why is he beating around the bush...? She took a calming breath. "Yes, I did. It's all over the news. But where are you now?"

"Me? I'm at the hospital. They are keeping me for observation... just for the night."

"Where is Ben? Is he with you?" She knew he wasn't from the way he was acting but she had to hear it before she would admit it to herself.

"Ben? Umm..."

At the end of her patience, she shouted into the phone. "Spit it out for cripes sake or I'll rip you a new asshole when I see you next!"

Her tirade caused everyone to look her way, including Ava, Kim, and Tim.

"Oh, oh..." Kim muttered.

"I'm on it," Ava replied. Spinning on her heel, she sprinted to her mom.

Abbi was apologizing to someone for her outburst when Ava arrived at the table. She motioned for her to give her the phone.

"Mark, I'm so sorry. I need answers and no one knows them... Ava wants to talk to you." Abbi handed Ava the phone as she got up from the table and headed to the washrooms. The only place she could escape to. Pushing open the first stall door, she locked it and sat heavily on the toilet, bursting into tears.

Carrying a tray full of drinks, Kim scanned the eating area for Abbi as she made her way to the table where Ava sat alone. "Where's your mom?" she asked, placing the tray on the table.

"She went to the washroom. I just got off the phone with Mark."

"And?" Kim hedged while she stuck straws in the drinks.

"He's in the hospital, just overnight... for observation. He should be released tomorrow if all goes well."

"Ok, so where did the plane go down?" Tim asked, dropping the bags of food on the table.

"Mark was told about 60 miles south of Gatlinburg Tennessee, near a little mountain town called Cooper's Hill."

"And Ben?" Waiting for Ava's response, Kim held her breath. She didn't know what they would do with Abbi if it wasn't good.

Ava took a deep breath. "Ben is nowhere to be found," she said, looking at Kim and Tim.

"What do you *mean*, nowhere to be *found?*" Abbi cried in horrified disbelief. Three shocked faces peered at her; it was clear that no one had seen her return. Abbi thrust out a shaky hand. "Give me my phone, Ava."

Concerned at her mother's current mental state, reluctantly, Ava passed her the phone. "Mom, Mark said he looked everywhere. And so did the police. It's like he just vanished into thin air."

By that time, Abbi wasn't listening. She tapped her screen, going instantly to the text messages... *Ben.* He had sent her two. The first she read with tears swimming in her eyes...

'Abbi. Love. It's me. Things are not looking so good for Mark and I and I won't go into detail. I know I have told you this before, but please, always remember that you captured my heart from the second we met. You are the best thing that has ever happened to me. I have no regrets with you, Abbi. No matter what happens, know that I will always love you and I'll always be by your side. Forever yours, Ben.'

She had to sit down as a soft sob escaped past her lips. Taking a steadying breath, she continued to read the second one...

'Hello there, Abbi, I presume? I am not sure who this is. But from the last message I sent you, I am confident that we know each other... on an intimate level. I seem to be in some need of aid but have no idea where I am. Can you please advise? Thanks, Benjamin Quinn.'

Abbi started giggling. Softly at first, then full out laughing hysterically. It really wasn't funny, of course, Ben having no clue who she was. But she couldn't help herself. She knew it! He was alive!

"What's so funny?" Tim asked.

Between the tears slipping down her cheeks and her hysterical laughing, everyone at the table thought she had finally lost it.

"Ahh..." She wiped the tears on her sleeve and said, "He's alive..."

"Mark is, yes... we know that mom."

Abbi shook her head; she shoved her phone to the center of the table. "Not Mark, Ava. Ben. He's alive." Grinning like a fool, she broke down in tears of joy and relief.

KIM WAS AT THE WHEEL as they headed towards the most southern city in Canada. Glancing in the rearview mirror at Abbi, she motioned at the car in front of them. "See, now isn't this much better than being chased by him?" True to his word, Tim was in the lead with sirens blaring and lights flashing. They were enroute to Windsor, just passing through Chatham Kent.

Abbi texted Ben back, after multiple attempts to reach him by phone had failed. Twenty minutes later he had responded, telling her that he was injured. A broken leg, he was sure of, and he was slipping in and out of consciousness. Abbi had at once called 911, who directed her to the authorities in Tennessee. She told them she was talking to Ben via text. They said they could contact his phone provider and narrow down the pings on the towers around the vicinity of the plane crash, but he had to make a call first. Her last text to him, she'd told him that it was imperative that he call her.

Abbi leaned her head back. She stared blankly at the night sky through the SUV's glass top roof, as it sped its way to their destination. Despite her protests, they'd decided to stay the night in Windsor; at least another forty-five-minute drive away. Luke and Lane were both out of town on business and so they had little choice but to stay in a hotel.

There were 9 hours, or more of driving ahead of them in the States. She hated to waste time on sleeping. She would see. She may just leave in the middle of the night, sneaking away like a thief... without Ava and Kim.

Chapter 2

B en woke with a start to find that a light dusting of snow covered him. *Where the hell am I? Now that's a question that may never get answered*, he thought wryly, as he laid a hand on his leg. He knew it was banged up bad, most likely broken. He also knew that if he didn't get out of there and soon, he wouldn't make it. If only he could find something that resembled a crutch, just maybe he could get the hell out of there. It would have to wait till daylight though. The moon barely gave off enough light to see through the leafless trees.

The sound of a twig snapping had him whipping his head around. Squinting, he looked but didn't see anything. But something was out there. He heard it, and he felt like he was being watched. Whatever it was, it didn't come close enough to get a good look at it. A raccoon likely. He hoped. Then again, he could have just imagined it. His mind had been playing tricks on him, since the second he had woken up laying on the forest floor. The first time, he'd heard a woman's voice. Ben had searched for her from his vantage point only to come to the realization it was only in his mind, it had him thinking that he was going crazy. Now, he looked forward to it.

He touched his fingers to the bump on his forehead, wincing from the pain. He tried to remember what had happened. He knew from the sickening screech of metal that played on repeat in his mind that he had been in a plane crash. From the looks of it, he had been the only occupant... or so he thought. It was the only thing he was certain of... that and his name.

Shivering against the cold, he closed his eyes, trying desperately to remember what his life was like. He had looked endlessly at the photos on his phone. There were pictures of a lake, a house in the middle of renovations, dogs. Pictures of him and a beautiful woman together, some of just her alone. He knew they were a couple; he could feel it in his gut, but he just couldn't remember her.

Abbi she was. The photo attached to her name and phone number told him so. He also knew deep down; she meant the world to him. Ben just wished he could remember her. The feel of her skin, her laugh, her voice, anything that would bring a hint of what he had meant to her. Did she love him? God, he hoped so. He could feel himself drifting off again. The image of Abbi burning into his mind was his last thought before sleep overtook him.

The buzzing of his phone had him jerking awake. It was Abbi. He squinted trying desperately to focus on the words in the text. *Ben, please call me. I need you to call. The police can trace your cell off the towers. But you have to call.*

He hit the phone icon as his teeth started to chatter. He waited shivering uncontrollably, praying the call would go through this time.

"Ben?"

He heard a soft voice in his ear. The same voice he had heard in his mind repeatedly.

Memories of her, of them, flashed through his mind "Abbi, is that you?" His voice broke on her name as it all came flooding back to him.

He could hear her crying softly. Like usual, her tears tore his heart out.

"Love, please don't cry. I'm fine. Just a bit banged up is all."

"You called me love, does that mean...?"

"Yeah, I remember. I could never forget you for long Abbi." He heard her let out a shaky breath, half laughing half crying. Ben remembered how beautiful she was with tears streaming down her face. He wanted nothing more than to kiss them away.

"Mark is in the hospital in Gatlinburg. Ava and Kim have no idea, but I'm on my way to you. They'll know once they wake up. I'm headed to the Detroit airport right now. Hang on a second." He heard a sharp whistle, and her hailing for a taxi. A muffling sound came through the speaker as she told her destination to the driver. "I'm back. I should be there in an hour and a half. I don't know, maybe more," she panted, out of breath.

Ben had no idea who Mark was, and who was Ava and Kim? Hell, he didn't even know who his own family was, for that matter. Maybe they were his family. All he knew at this point was Abbi and she was coming for him.

"Wait, you're going to fly... alone?" he asked her.

Softly, Abbi said, "Nothing is stopping me from getting to you."

The determination in her voice made his heart swell. Knowing what she was about to embark on, he loved her more in that moment than he had ever loved another.

Swallowing hard, he said, "Abbi, I'm about to pass out I think...." He lied, wanting to spare her from his emotions. He hated to end the call, but he had to.

"Ben... No!! Stay with me! Don't you dare fall asleep on me now!"

He had to chuckle at the fire in her voice.

"Fine, just keep talking to me. Tell me what you've been up to. I'll try to stay awake. It's just so bloody cold out here." He mumbled, just as he heard the crack of branches breaking. *Good god, I hope she didn't hear that...*

But she had. "What the hell was that?!" she screeched in his ear. He could feel the panic in her voice rising with each word through the phone.

Lights blinded Ben. He had no idea what it was other than it was a vehicle with a loud muffler.

"One second love," he muttered. He quickly switched his phone to record, stuffing it and Abbi's muffled curses into his pocket.

"See, Dean, I told you it was that Hollywood actor, sitting here in the middle of these here trees."

How the hell did they find me? All Ben could see in any direction was endless forest. At that point he didn't care, he would be back to civilization soon.

He could make out two figures. The one talking, skinny as a bean pole. The one called Dean, was tall as well but built like an athlete. Relief spread through Ben; he was saved. It came as a bit of a shock that they thought he was an actor though. The thought sounded absurd to his rattled mind.

"For once in your pathetic life Smitty, you're right. Come on. Let's get him loaded into the back of the truck." The one called Dean stalked over to Ben.

"Uh, how do you know me?" Ben asked the one named Smitty.

Smitty snorted. "Man, there isn't a person in the world who doesn't know who you are."

Ben grimaced as the two men hoisted him up by the armpits. "I see," he panted, out of breath.

Dean shot Smitty a look. "That's a lie, I didn't."

"Ignore him. Can you walk?" Smitty asked, trying to steady Ben.

"How dumb can you be? The man has been sitting here for hours. If he could walk, he would have left by now." Dean spat out at his companion as he gathered debris from the plane wreckage.

Smitty shrugged his shoulders as he put an arm around Ben's waist. "Don't pay him no mind." He muttered under his breath, "He's just pissed you landed in the middle of our farm."

Ben glanced around as he hobbled to the pickup truck and frowned. *Farm? All I can see is barren trees for miles. What the hell kind of farm is it?*

"Smitty, keep your trap shut." Dean growled as he brought up the rear.

He walked to the bed of the truck and tossed his findings inside. He yanked on the driver's door and grumbled, "We don't want Mr. Hollywood knowing anything... got it? Otherwise, he may go missing again."

"Sorry." Smitty darted his eyes to Ben as he opened the door of the club cab for him. Both men knew what 'missing' meant.

Ben climbed into the backseat trying his damnedest to keep from bumping his leg. It was impossible for him not to grunt in pain when he settled on the seat.

Turning in his seat, Dean looked at Ben. "What's up with you?"

With sweat beading on his brow, Ben pulled on his pant leg, tugging on it he pulled his leg into the truck and grimaced. "Busted my leg in the crash,"

Dean sent him a sour look. "Great, just what we needed."

"We can take him to the hospital." Smitty looked to Dean for confirmation. "Right?"

"Nope. Too much of a risk, someone is bound to recognize him."

Smitty tried to reason. "We can't leave him to suffer."

"We'll get Murdock to look at him," Dean said and started the truck. Moving the gear shift, he backed up. "If she can't set it, well that's just too bad, isn't it?"

Everyone fell silent as they sped through the forest. Ben searched the scenery, tree after tree, his hope of finding a landmark he could tell Abbi about slowly came to a dismal halt.

He cocked his head when he heard someone yelling from what sounded like far off in the distance. It wasn't someone, it was Abbi.

Shit!

He forgot she was still on the phone, no doubt hearing every word exchanged. He quickly put his hand over his jeans pocket, fearing she would be heard by the two in the front seat. By feel, he disconnected the call. He couldn't afford for them to find out he had it if he wanted to be found.

The truck slowed down and pulled up to what looked like an abandoned warehouse in the middle of a clearing.

This does not look good.

Dean killed the engine, looking over at Smitty and jerked his head to the back seat where Ben sat.

"Get him inside, take him to Murdock. See if he can be fixed up."

"And if he can't? Then do we take him to the hospital?"

"I don't know yet; I'll have to think about it. He should bring in a hefty price." Dean sneered.

Price? What the hell are they dealing here?

Smitty nodded. "Right." He opened his door and slammed it shut.

He opened Ben's door, and said, "Come on, I'll get you looked at." Again, Ben couldn't help but groan in pain as Smitty helped him from the truck to the building. The slightest movement of his leg made him want to vomit.

The smell caught Ben off guard. His first thought was that a family of skunks had taken up residence close by. As they drew closer to the building, the smell only intensified.

Smitty guided Ben to a post. "Here, hang onto this while I open the door."

He gripped it with one hand and waited. He wished he could just take off running. But he had a feeling that if he tried to, a bullet would find its way into the back of his head. Nope. Better to play it smart, he had Abbi coming for him.

Funny, how a few months ago he wouldn't have even cared. He remembered somewhat of his life before Abbi came into it. Merely existing. Amazing how she'd changed it.

The sound of Smitty shoving open the huge sliding door brought his thoughts back to the present.

Hooking an arm around Ben's waist, Smitty said, "Come on, let's get you inside."

Ben's eyes grew large as they crossed into the light streaming from the open doorway. That wasn't a family of skunks he smelled a few minutes ago. That was the farm. He let out a low whistle. Before him, row after row, was the largest marijuana plants he'd seen in his life. He had no clue where he was, but he was sure that what was before him was an illegal grow op.

"Bloody hell..." The seriousness of his current predicament hit him like a ton of bricks.

"Pretty impressive, huh?" Smitty asked smiling, as he closed the door with a loud bang.

"Indeed, it is." Ben returned as he watched a worker walking around with a gun. One that he was sure was loaded. *No. this wasn't good, not good at all.*

The stakes just got higher. He had to come up with a plan and damn quick if he was ever going to get out of this alive....

Chapter 3

"Ben! Please answer me!" Abbi screamed frantically into her phone. "Damn it!!"

God, she felt so helpless. When she heard the crashing of trees and the sound of the vehicle, hope flared in her chest. She thought for sure the police had found him. That hope soon plummeted to her gut after hearing the voices. She held her breath as she heard them talk about Ben... not to him. Abbi instantly had a bad feeling about them. She had repeatedly called out to him, praying he would respond. The only one to hear her was the cab driver who was sending startled glances in the rearview mirror at her.

Just clearing customs at the border, Abbi sat there listening to the muffled conversation on her cell. Not being able to stand it any longer, she leaned forward and said, "Can you step on it, please?"

"Sure thing, ma'am." The taxi shot forward as the driver stomped on the gas pedal.

"Sweet baby Jesus, not that fast. I need to get there in one piece."

The driver mumbled an apology as he slowed down.

Abbi felt relieved as the car reduced its speed to a more reasonable pace. She needed to call the police in Gatlinburg, but she dared not hang up on Ben.

"Ah, sir." Abbi tapped the driver on the shoulder. "Do you have a cell phone I can use?"

He looked at her as if she had horns growing out of her head. "Lady, you do realize you're talking on one, right?"

"Yes, I do, but I can't just hang up on him!" She bit that out a little louder than she intended. *Calm your jets Abbi, he has no clue what's going on...*

She tried again, more calmly this time, "I'm sorry to ask but it's a matter of life and death!" She saw the doubt he cast her way in the rear-view mirror.

"Look, my boyfriend was in a plane crash in the middle of butt fu... um a forest. He's been missing since yesterday morning. And these..." she waved her hand about, as if she were at a loss for the correct term "... people showed up."

"Well, that's a good thing, right?"

"Yes ... *No!*!" She denied vehemently. "They aren't there to help him! They're there to take him!!" She was close to snapping.

"How can you be so sure? I mean, if it were me, and people showed up I would be pretty damn happy to see them... Wouldn't you?" The cabbie reasoned.

Shaking her head, she all but yelled. "Yes! If they were the right people, *but these people aren't the right people!*" she ended on a hurried hiss.

He gave her a confused look; she had to explain.

"I know this because, I heard them. They are going to sell him or kill him... I'm not sure which. But whatever it is, it's not a good thing." She paused, listening into her phone to what sounded like Ben groaning in pain. "*Oh my God, what the hell are they doing to him?*"

"Lady, I think you're overreacting."

Me overreact?

Abbi wasn't that person to throw her name around to get what she wanted. In fact, she never did. But this was calling for drastic measures.

"Look..." She squinted in thought. "What was your name again?"

"It's Leo." He smiled. "But I never told you, my name."

Huh, he's a nice-looking man when he doesn't think I'm crazy, Abbi thought to herself.

"Leo, my name is Abbi Stevens." She used her pen name in hopes he would recognize it. She held her hand out by way of introduction.

Never taking his eyes off the road, he reached over and took her hand for a quick shake. "Nice to meet you, Abbi." He nodded; the smile was replaced with that 'this lady is crazy' look again.

Great, he has no clue who I am. She had no choice but to pull out the big guns.

"Ah, you see. My boyfriend... Ben Everett, you know, the actor?" She arched a brow, waiting to see the dawning recognition his name would bring to Leo's face. It never happened. "The one that was in the plane crash, well... It's been all over the news I'm sure you heard by now."

He shook his head. "Nope, can't say I've heard of him, and I don't listen to the news."

Does this guy live under a rock on his off days?

"Ok." Abbi counted to ten. "How about movies, do you watch movies?"

"Sure do! I don't tell people this because they would think I'm crazy, a big bear of a guy like me. But seeing how you're already crazy, I'll tell ya. I do love a good chick flick." Leo grinned at her reflection in the mirror.

Abbi rolled her eyes. "Of course you do." She flung herself back against the seat and let out an exasperated sigh of defeat. Knowing that Ben had never been in a movie made for women, Leo wouldn't know him even if he was standing in the same room.

She tuned him out, straining to hear any sign that Ben was still connected to her. A rumbling, squealing noise came over the airwaves that didn't sound good.

She was trying to picture what could have made that noise when Leo's prattling broke her thoughts.

"Now, that Mark Donovan, he's quite the character." He laughed smacking his knee.

"What... *wait!*" This was her chance to seize the moment. She leaned forward, all but hanging over the front seat. "Mark! I know him! He rents out my house."

Leo snickered. "Sure, he does lady."

"He does!" Taking the phone from her ear, Abbi swiped through her photos, careful not to disconnect her call. Finally, she found one of Mark, with Ava and Kim.

Shoving it under his nose she said, "Here, look. That's him with my sister and daughter."

"Whoa, hang on a minute, let me pull over before I crash into something." Leo signaled, veering to the shoulder, he brought the car to a rolling stop.

Putting the cell back to her ear, Abbi grabbed the door handle, and shoved it open. Kicking it shut, she yanked open the front door and planted her butt on the seat. She would get better results if she were eye to eye with the man.

Leo jumped back in his seat; surprise registered on his face. Abbi threw him a smile as she settled in and closed the door with a soft thud.

She could tell he wasn't too sure about her, especially now.

Shooting her a wary look, Leo motioned with his hand. "Ok, let me see your phone."

Abbi had heard nothing for a while, but just in case, she switched the speaker on so that she could listen for Ben while they scrolled through her photos.

"Huh... so you do." Leo shrugged, "So, what's he really like?"

"Wouldn't you like to know," Abbi said airily and folded her arms across her chest. She leaned back and looked out her window.

He nodded at her phone as he pulled away from the curb. "Look Abbi, you can't just show me these, and just leave me hanging," he said. Looking at her, he noted her defiant stance. "Fine! Okay!! I'll let you use my phone, but only if you tell me."

Abbi stuck her hand out. "Phone first, then I tell you everything you want to know."

"Deal." He took her offered hand and shook it as he passed the phone to her with the other. She greedily took it, and quickly called the Gatlinburg Sheriff's office.

Abbi had just finished telling Leo about Mark when he pulled the cab to stop at the curb outside the airport.

"Well, it was real nice chatting with you Abbi. You got my number, right?" That was the fifth time he asked her.

I bet it was, Abbi thought, nodding in answer to his question. She had told him everything about Mark, right down to his favourite food. She would have to tell Mark that she was sorry, to the point of grovelling if she had to.

Somehow Leo had not only gleaned every detail out of her, but he swindled a promise of a trip to Pearl Lake to meet Mark when everything was sorted out.

"It was nice talking to you too Leo, thanks again for letting me use your phone." She tossed a couple of crisp one hundred-dollar bills at him before slamming her door shut.

Leo rolled down the window and said, "Abbi, you gave me too much."

"I know I did." She looked at him over her shoulder, and said, "Keep the change." Raising her had in a wave, she hurried inside. She power walked through the terminal and marched up to the attendant, paid for her ticket, then ran to the terminal gate to catch her flight. Crossing onto the bridge, she slowed her pace, trying to catch her breath. If all went well, she would be in Tennessee within an hour or so. She could only hope she didn't end up running down the aisle like the crazy woman Leo thought she was.

Abbi hoped she appeared calm and confidant to others. That was the furthest thing from the truth. Her feet felt like they wanted to take root, she felt the weight of anxiety with every step she took. Wanting nothing more than to turn around and head back to the safety of the terminal; she forged on; she had to... Ben needed her.

Taking the first step onto the airplane, Abbi took a deep breath, trying to calm the anxiety building within. She found her seat and planted herself in it, buckling the belt as tight as she could. *As if this flimsy thing will save me,* she thought as her stomach churned.

She sat staring straight ahead at the seat in front of her. Praying that the plane would stay in the air and that she wouldn't make a complete ass of herself. Leaning back, she closed her eyes. Memories of the last time she had flown came flooding back. It was to Madrid with Ben. He was needed back to film the last scenes for the Jasper Killings, and oh what a time she had on that flight...

She had been drunk, of course. He made sure she stayed in her seat the whole time. He even went as far as holding her when she started keening like a baby and held her hair as she threw up in the aisle. Tears fell silently down her cheeks. Missing him was one thing, but him being taken somewhere, only God knew, was slowly tearing her apart second by second.

"You're flying Economy? Really Abbi. Just what the hell are you thinking?"

Abbi cracked open an eye at the familiar voice of her sister Kim, only to discover Ava and an out of uniform Tim, all standing in the aisle gaping at her.

"Mom, are you crazy? You can't fly alone," Ava said, sitting in the seat beside her.

Abbi felt like a child being scolded. "I can so and there is nothing wrong with Economy it's still the same plane and I can still get drunk. Might as well save a dollar or two." To be honest, she was relieved to see them. She hadn't really wanted to take to the skies alone. Or at all for the matter. "How did you find me, anyway? And Tim? You can't just leave work," she said, tiredly.

"Sure I can, Abbi. I'm on vacation as we speak." He smiled. "What better way to spend it than looking for a missing person?"

Kim jerked her thumb at Tim. "Mr. Cop here... followed us from the hotel," Kim said as she dropped to the seat behind her, across the aisle. "We flew past you on the way here. Surprised you didn't see Ava waving at you like a fool, hanging out the window like she was."

Abbi took Ava's hand, giving it a squeeze. "Well, thanks for coming. I didn't want to wake you two up, that's why I snuck out."

"Snuck out?" Kim snorted. "Is that what you call it? Cussing and muttering to yourself as you banged out the door, isn't exactly how one would sneak."

Kim looked up when she felt someone standing out of her field of vison. A man stood holding a carry on and his ticket. "Yeah?" she asked.

"Ah... excuse me. I think this is my seat."

Kim looked at the seat she was sitting on. "Hmm, nope, looks like I'm sitting in it."

The man said. "You can't just pick any seat you want."

"Ah." Kim leaned forward and nodded. "I think I did. Here." She smacked her boarding pass on his chest and took his ticket. "It's first class, go have fun."

The man looked at the ticket and without a word, and a spring to his step he was off to first class.

"You can't just do that," Tim said, still standing in the aisle.

"Sure I can." Kim grabbed his ticket and turned to the woman sitting beside her. "Want a first-class spot?"

"No?" the lady answered.

"Yes, you do. Here." She passed Tim's ticket to the woman and said, "They wait on you hand a foot. Go have fun."

The woman sat for a full minute then got up and gathered her belongings. Shrugging she looked at Tim and said, "Why not? Thanks!"

"Why not indeed," Tim grinned and settled in the vacated seat just as the pilot's voice came over the speaker announcing takeoff.

Abbi gripped the arms on her seat, leaned back and bit her lip as sweat beaded on her brow. She squeezed her eyes tightly shut. *Okay, Abbi calm the hell down, it's only for a few minutes and then it'll even out.*

"Hang in there, mom." Ava spoke to her in a soothing tone. "I'll get you a nice stiff drink in a minute."

"You should have started drinking when you left the hotel," Kim cackled. For some reason, she always thought it was hilarious how Abbi reacted to flying.

Abbi clenched her jaw and muttered out the side of her mouth. "Will you just shut the hell up, Kim."

The plane finally evened out, allowing her to relax the grip she had on the seat. Thank God it was a short flight. When she got Ben back, they were driving home... alone.

Chapter 4

S mitty grabbed Ben by the arm and wrapped it around his shoulders. "Come on, I'll get you over to Murdock. See if she can help your leg." He guided Ben to a short hallway. Taking a left, they came to a doorway at the end of the hall.

"Hey Murdock," Smitty called out. "Got a minute? This guy needs looking at."

Ben saw a tiny woman who had to be at least eighty, hunched over a microscope. He doubted she could patch him up; she looked so weak and nothing like a doctor. She turned just then, scrutinizing him over her glasses. She motioned with a wave of her hand at the table sitting in the middle of the room.

"Help him up."

Ben swallowed hard. Bloody hell, her voice sounded as old as she looked. He wasn't entirely sure he trusted her but had little choice. The pain was blinding; every move had him fighting consciousness and the urge to vomit.

She shuffled over to him. "What's your name boy?"

"Ben," he answered, grimacing as he pulled his leg up and onto the table. He could feel the beads of sweat forming on his upper lip at the effort. Heaven help him, he felt like sawing his own leg off.

"My name's Daisy, Daisy Murdock. Now let's have a look see." She pulled a pair of scissors from her pocket and made fast work of cutting his pants at the ankle, clear up to his hip. She let out a low whistle, nearly spitting out her dentures in the process.

"Oh, hell, No!" Daisy said. "Smitty, go tell Dean there's no way I can fix that." She backed away, shaking her head. Quickly she ran behind Ben, hurling into the nearby sink as Smitty took off out the door gagging.

What the hell kind of doctor can't set a leg? Ben wondered. He looked down at it. Aside from it being bloody from a scrape and bruised, it wasn't that bad. Sure, the bone bulged against his skin, but at least it hadn't poked through... yet. Yeah, it was gross but Ben had seen worse. Something was off with this doctor.

Ben twisted around to get a look at her face. "Um, Daisy? Are you okay?"

She cleared her throat and snapped. "Yeah, what makes you think I'm not?"

Ben pursed his lips. "Oh, I don't know... Maybe tossing your cookies at the sight of my leg has me wondering."

Daisy wiped her mouth with the back of her hand.

Ben noticed something very odd about her. "Huh..." he said, squinting in thought.

"What?!" She squeaked. "Why are you looking at me like that?"

"Your hands." He nodded towards them. "They don't match your face."

Ben was certain that Daisy Murdock was not who she claimed to be. In fact, he would bet on it. For one, her voice suddenly changed from the soft whispers of an old lady to a young, scared woman. He had to admit, her appearance was very convincing though. To the untrained eye, one would never be able to tell. Too bad for her that he'd seen right through it. *Wait a second, how the hell do I know that?* He frowned, searching what little memory he had. Nothing.

Daisy interrupted his thoughts. "What can I say, I use a lot of hand lotion. Look, I know who you are," she said quietly.

Ben shot her a brooding glance. "You do?"

"Yeah, who doesn't?" Daisy silently moved to the door, closing it softly. Turning to look at him she said, "You're Ben Quinn. Everyone, at some point in their life, has seen a movie you're in."

Ben just sat there nodding, he had no clue if she were right, his memory just wouldn't reach back that far.

"You have no clue, do you?" Daisy asked. Reaching up, she grabbed his chin, turning his head to look at the bump on his forehead.

"Is it that obvious?" He'd need to work on that. If she could tell, then so could the others. He couldn't risk them finding out. Doing so, would put him in more of a perilous situation than he already was.

"Mhm," she said, walking over to a cupboard, she took the first aid kit and returned to his side.

Soaking a cotton ball in peroxide, she looked at him, "This will sting."

"Go ahead, it can't hurt any worse than my leg."

She wiped the bump so hard, it felt like she was trying to flatten it with the cotton.

He winced. "Bloody hell woman! Can you not do that? Give it to me. I'll do it myself." Ben took the cotton ball from her and wiped his wound with it. Baiting her, he said, "You know, for someone so old, you have a heavy hand."

Daisy gave a tight smile. "Ah about that..."

Ben held up his hand. "No need to say a word. The less I know the better."

The door opened and in stepped Smitty with Dean close on his heels. The old woman in Daisy suddenly returned.

"Murdock, Smitty says you can't set his leg?" Dean barked.

"Take a look at it and ask me that question again," she retorted.

Dean moved over to where Ben was on the table, all color drained from his face.

"Well, shit!!"

"I told you it was bad," Smitty said to Dean, his eyes never wavering from the sight of Ben's leg. "He needs a hospital and fast," he said the obvious.

"Well, he's not going anywhere tonight." Dean looked Ben in the eyes. "You're damn lucky Smitty, and Daisy found you earlier. There's a freak snowstorm happening out there right now. No one would have found you in time."

Found me earlier? Ben wanted to question that but kept his mouth shut.

Daisy nodded, her eyes growing large as she took in the bruising on Ben's skin. "I can wrap it but that's about it. He's likely going to need surgery for that bone." She tore her eyes away to get a tensor bandage. Turning to Ben, she said, "I should probably take your boot off, do you think you can handle the pain?"

Ben nodded.

"Lay back in case you pass out. Smitty, hold his thigh down, Dean hold his shoulders."

Daisy quickly undid his boot, slowly she slipped it off his foot. It felt like ice. She grabbed a pen and ran it along the underside of Ben's foot. "Can you feel that?" she questioned him.

"I feel a slight tingling sensation. Why?"

Daisy looked at Dean and shook her head. Smitty caught the exchange between the two. He could see the panic in Ben's face. "Uh, nothing, buddy, you're gonna be fine, isn't he Murdock?"

She shook her head no but said, "Yeah, just fine." She quickly wrapped his leg from foot to thigh. He hardly had any feeling in his foot. She was no doctor, but she knew enough to know that Ben could be in serious trouble.

"So now what?" Smitty asked. "Where is he gonna bunk tonight?" He looked at Dean for an answer.

Daisy spoke up. "He's staying with me for the night in my cabin. I... Uh... I need to monitor him."

None of the men made a noise about that. Ben knew there was something wrong with his leg, but serious enough to need surgery... he highly doubted that.

To have hardly any feeling, just a slight tingle in his foot was not right, especially when Daisy had a heavy hand. But he could feel his pulse, it was swollen, and it did just happen. Of course, it would be numb for a few days at least.

"Help Ben sit up," Daisy said to the two men. "I've got some crutches in the supply room. Go get them, will you Dean."

Ben noticed that she tended to order people around. It had him wondering if she was the boss of the whole operation.

"Smitty, I'll need your help getting him to my cabin. He can use the crutches, that is, if he has the strength." She looked to Ben. "You do have the strength, don't you?"

"Yeah, I'll be fine." He nodded. He wanted nothing more than to get the hell out of there and to the cabin. He was in dire need of food and a decent sleep.

"Good. But just in case, Smitty you can be there to pick him up if he falls."

Helping Ben off the table, Smitty said, "Sure thing Murdock. I'll be right by his side."

"Come on then, let's get out of here." Daisy grabbed a jacket and gently pulled it on as if she were in a great deal of pain. She led the way, down the hall and to the left. Pushing the door open, she was almost thrown back from the force of the wind. Blowing snow blinded them momentarily as they all filed outside.

"Follow me!" Daisy shouted over the howling wind. Ben hobbled after her with Smitty bringing up the rear.

One step at a time, Ben repeated like a mantra in his mind. His arms felt like they would give out any second. The crutches slipped a few times, but he was able to catch himself before falling face first into the snowdrifts. Daisy finally reached the small cabin, she flung the door open, holding it for the two men to enter.

"Damnation! This weather is nuts," she said slamming the door closed behind them.

Ben chanced a look around. The room was rustic and simple. A small fireplace sat squarely against one wall with a sofa opposite. A small kitchen area with a table and two chairs sat off to one side. Ben could see two doors, leading to what he presumed was a bedroom and bathroom.

"Calvin, can you help Ben over to the table there?" Daisy said as she threw a newspaper-wrapped log into the fireplace and lit a match to it.

Ben gawked at her then at Smitty. *Wait... did I just hear her right? Who the hell is Calvin?*

"Sure thing, Sam. Here Ben, take a seat." Smitty pulled out a chair, as Ben sat down with a heavy sigh.

"Want a coffee?" Smitty asked as he filled the kettle. "I'll make you something to eat too. You must be starved."

Daisy sat down opposite Ben. She looked to Smitty. "I'll take a coffee too please," she murmured as she picked at her jawline.

For a minute, Ben thought he was hallucinating. First, the two were calling each other by different names and now it looked like Daisy was pulling her face off.

Ben rubbed his eyes; he knew he was extremely tired, or maybe he was asleep, and this was all just a nightmare?

Nope, he wasn't sleeping. Her face was now bare. And what it revealed was a pretty young woman with a sprinkling of freckles across her cheeks.

He watched in disbelief as she pulled out a set of fake teeth, tossing them in a water filled bowl that sat in the middle of the table. Ben gawked in revulsion as water splattered on its surface.

Daisy glanced at him. The look on his face must have been priceless because she burst out laughing, "Sorry about this, but we need to have a chat."

Ben nodded in agreement. This was getting more bizarre by the second....

Chapter 5

A short hour later their flight was taxiing down the runway at the Gatlinburg airport. Abbi surprisingly wasn't drunk. A little tipsy, but not drunk. After knocking back a shot of gin and a glass of wine, she felt somewhat capable of handling the flight. That was until they were met with a little turbulence half-way through. For the rest of it, she sat there with her head between her knees, ready for impact at any second. Impact from what, she wasn't entirely sure, but at least she was ready.

"Mom? Are you okay?" Ava asked, rubbing her back soothingly. "You can sit up now. We are almost at the terminal."

She sat up and leaned back in her seat.

"Abbi what the hell happened to you?" Kim chuckled.

"What do you mean?"

"Here, look." Kim laughed as she passed her phone to her.

Abbi saw in the mirrored back of the cellphone case her reflection. Her makeup was smudged, and her hair was pushed forward. Sticking straight out, it framed her face. She looked like she had been sitting the entire flight on the wing of the plane, backwards. The whole look reminded her of a windswept clown.

Abbi lifted a shoulder. "Meh, I don't care at this point." She passed Kim her phone back as she gathered her purse and carry on. All she cared about was finding Ben.

THEY HAD CHECKED INTO a hotel close to the hospital and were now walking to the nurses' station on the floor Mark's room was on. They had no idea if they were even allowed to come at such a late hour, but they had to try. While they did, Tim had gone to the local sheriffs to find out as much information he could on where the plane had crashed.

His plan was to make a map of the area and backtrack from the crash site.

"Excuse me, could you tell me which room Mark Donovan is in?" Ava asked.

Abbi glanced over to see a woman sitting behind the counter of the nurse's station on her cellphone; clearly ignoring Ava.

Kim bristled. "Move over Ava." Kim tapped the counter impatiently, trying to get the woman's attention. "Hey there! We're here to see Mark Donovan. What room is he in?"

The lady glanced up. "He's in a private room and is not having any visitors." Tiredly she pointed to the clock on the wall. "Especially at midnight."

She then turned her attention back to her phone, chuckling as she typed vigorously. It made Abbi fuming mad. At this point, she had had enough. Nudging Kim aside, she stepped forward. "Look lady, we have travelled all the way from northern Ontario and Mark is expecting us. So, if you don't want us to go into each room looking for him, waking people up, you better tell us what room he's in."

The nurse clearly annoyed, looked up at Abbi and let out a small gasp.

Suddenly the nurse came to a half stand as she stared at Abbi. "Abbi Stevens?"

Abbi blinked a few times. "What?"

Kim elbowed her in the ribs, while she jerked her head towards the nurse. "Ah... Why yes, I'm Abbi Stevens." She pasted a charming smile on her lips. "And you are?"

"My name's Cindy. I'm a huge fan of the Jasper Killings. Can you sign my book? I have it right here." Cindy quickly rummaged in her bag, producing the book along with a pen.

She was surprised at how fast Cindy could move when she wanted something. "Ah, sure." Abbi took both in hand and scribbled her name. "Look, I'm sorry for my outburst a minute ago, it's just been a really long day."

"Oh, don't you worry about that! I understand completely." Cindy grinned as she glanced at Abbi's signature.

"What room did you say Mark was in again?" Abbi asked sweetly, knowing full well she didn't say.

Cindy hurriedly came around the counter. "He's in room 304. Here let me take you ladies right to him. I'm sure he will be happy to see you."

"How kind of you," Kim sneered.

Abbi shot her a look as they followed Cindy down the hall, silently communicating to Kim to shut up.

They made their way to a set of double doors marked 'Private'. Cindy scanned her key card and pushed one of the doors open, holding it for them to join her. As they continued down the hall Abbi glanced at each open doorway, half expecting to see Mark lying in a bed. Finally, they came to a stop; room 304.

The nurse gave a quick rap with her knuckles on the gleaming wood. "Mr. Donovan, are you decent?" She asked above a whisper. "You have some visitors." Cindy smiled, opening it wide for them to enter.

Abbi smiled at her. "Thank you for being so helpful."

Kim chimed in. "Yes! Thank you *so* much!"

Cindy nodded and quietly closed the door behind her.

"Did you really have to be such a bitch to her?" Abbi bit out.

"Look who's talking Miss *'Look lady, we've travelled blah blah blah...'*" Kim laughed.

Cutting between the two of them, her eyes flashed daggers, Ava said, "Enough!!"

"Ladies."

All eyes turned to the man in the bed.

Ava rushed over to give him a hug. "Oh my gosh, Mark! We're sorry, it's been an awfully long trip."

For once, Kim had the decency to look ashamed. "Hey Mark." She gave him a small wave. "How are you doing?"

"Good, good." He nodded and smiled; a sad one that didn't reach his eyes.

Abbi had never felt so empty. Yes, she was happy to see Mark, to see him alive and well. But heaven help her, it hurt so damn much knowing that Ben wasn't there with him. Tears started to well in her eyes.

Mark held his arms wide. "Come here, sweets."

She walked to his bed in a daze, collapsing in his arms as her body wracked with sobs.

"I'm so sorry Abbi. I searched for him everywhere. I couldn't find him. It's like he just disappeared." Mark's voice broke. "One way or another, come tomorrow we are going to go look for him and find him. I promise."

Abbi nodded. Pulling away, she sniffled. "It's okay. I know you looked for him." She wiped her tears away with her sleeve. It just occurred to her Mark didn't know she had talked to Ben.

She gave him a watery smile. "He's alive Mark."

A pained look crossed over Mark's face. "Abbi. You know that may not be the case, right?"

"No. He really is. Ben sent me a text. He didn't know who I was but knew from our conversations that I meant something to him. He called me, too." She began to pace. The relief she felt when she heard his voice. He remembered, how, she had no idea; but the feeling of hearing him, was one she couldn't put into words.

"That's fantastic news!" Mark was ecstatic. "What did he say? Did he say where he was?"

She stopped to look at him. "No, he didn't say where he was. I think in the middle of a forest." She began to pace again. "Someone has him. I heard them come through. It sounded like a big truck plowing down branches and trees." She heaved a sigh and looked at Ava and Kim, "I didn't tell any of you this. But whoever took Ben... it didn't sound good. He can't walk."

"What do you mean he can't walk?" Kim asked, frowning as she sat down in a chair.

"Ben said his leg is broken or at least he thinks it is. And I assumed he must have hit his head because he didn't remember me at first," she said, rubbing her own forehead. "Anyway, there were two guys talking... Smitty and Dean. They didn't talk to him, but about him. The one seemed like he wanted to help... Smitty I think it was, wanted to take him to a hospital. Dean said that Murdock could look at him..." She trailed off. Not wanting to repeat what she'd heard for fear of it coming true.

"And???" They all said in unison.

Abbi turned to look at them, expectant eyes stared back at her. "And..." She swallowed hard, trying so desperately to push the swell of tears down her throat. "There was mention of a farm. I'm not sure what kind of farm would be in a forest?" She was stalling; she knew it. Deciding that there was no reason to not tell them, she simply said, "And Dean said, 'We don't want Mr. Hollywood knowing anything, or he may just go missing again'. But the way he said missing, he... he um, didn't mean missing." Suddenly, she felt sick.

Abbi ran to a door tucked into the wall, and shoved it open, thankful that it was a washroom. She fell to her knees, leaned over the toilet, and retched her guts out. When the worst of it was over, she shakily sat on the floor, leaned against the wall, and hugged her knees to her. Taking a lungful of breath, she pushed the thoughts of how many germs she just came across. God, she hated throwing up in a toilet, especially in strange one.

Wiping a hand over her mouth, she pulled her cell phone from her pocket and opened her texts to Ben. She so wanted to call him but didn't dare. If someone heard his phone ring, or heard him talking, she was sure they would take it from him. It was 2 am and she needed to sleep; otherwise, she would be of no use to anyone. She decided to send him a quick text; he always left his cell on vibrate; it would be safe.

'*Ben, It's Abbi. We are here in Tennessee. Just leaving Mark's hospital room, will text you once we get to the hotel. Please be safe. I miss you dreadfully. Love Abbi*'

She hit the send button and she stood up. Opening the door she said, "Guys I need some sleep and I'm sure Mark does, too."

"Yeah, me too," Kim said. "Mark, we will come by in the morning to get you, okay?"

"I'll be here." He nodded as her and Ava went out into the hall. "Abbi. Can you look in my jacket pocket it's hanging in the closet." He motioned to the door to the right of his bed.

"Um... sure. What am I looking for?" she asked as she pulled the door open.

"A box, a small one... But don't look in it." He rushed to say.

Abbi glanced at him; confusion etched on her face.

"Promise me you won't open it."

Her hand closed around the box and froze. She gave a quick nod. "I promise, Mark." She pulled her hand from his jacket and looked down at what it held. There in her palm, was a small black box. One that would hold a ring...

She shook her head as tears sprung to her eyes. "Mark. I can't..."

"Abbi... yes you can," he softly replied. "I made a promise to Ben. That no matter what..." He stopped and swallowed back the tears forming in his throat. "You just hold on to that until you see him again, and I know you will. Then, you give it to him."

It's what Ben wanted. Otherwise, he would never have given it to Mark. Abbi nodded.

"Okay. I'll do that." Her voice betrayed her as it broke on the last word. She made her way to the door, then stopped to look back towards the bed.

"Mark? It's not your fault, you know that, right?" She knew he was feeling guilty.

"Yeah, I know. "He turned away to look out the window at the night sky. "I'll see you in the morning, Abbi."

"I'll see you in the morning."

She walked out the door to join the others waiting in the hall.

Mark couldn't help but feel guilty. The memory of his last moments with Ben, his words, echoing in his mind.

"I had to send Abbi a text. To tell her one last time that I love her."

He had scoffed at Ben. He had been having his own doubts, but to hear Ben voice them...

"Man, everything will be fine. We will be back home in no time. And you can ask her to marry you, just as you planned."

They had hugged then. He had felt Ben put something in his pocket and known what it was. He remembered looking at Ben and wondered what the man was thinking. Afterall they were on the same plane.

"Promise me you'll give that to Abbi... if I don't make it."

"Come on Ben don't talk like that. You keep it..."

"Promise me Mark."

Had Ben had a premonition?

"Alright! I promise buddy..."

After what Abbi said she'd heard, he wasn't sure they would find Ben, and if they did... would he be alive?

Chapter 6

"Here, Ben." Smitty passed him a steaming mug and set a plate of sandwiches on the table.

"Thanks man. So, uh... do one of you mind telling me what's going on?" Ben asked, reaching for a sandwich.

"Well, as you can see, we are sitting smack dab in the middle of a grow op... an illegal one, I might add." Daisy sighed, looking to Smitty. At his nod, she continued. "And we aren't who we appear to be."

Ben squinted, chewing thoughtfully. *That was obvious.*

Smitty cleared his throat. "If we tell you who we are... you have to play along."

Ben pursed his lips and shrugged. "Sure. Why not? It can't get any worse." He noticed the dark look pass across Smitty's face.

Great, just, great. "Okay... It can, can't it?" Ben looked between Smitty and Daisy for confirmation.

Both nodded slowly. Daisy got up and went to check the windows and doors. Making sure all was locked tight, she turned to Ben.

"I'm Special Agent Sam Perkins with the FBI." She inclined her head towards Smitty. "And that is Special Agent Calvin Falls with the DEA. As you've probably guessed, we are working undercover. Have been for roughly four months."

Calvin spoke up. "It's vital that you remember to use our fictitious names."

"Then why the hell did you tell me!" Ben asked.

"When your plane went down. Our agencies put the call out for us to be on the lookout for any missing passengers. All have been accounted for but you Ben. And given your celebrity status, we decided it was in your best interest..." Sam paused, taking a deep breath, she continued. "We believe your plane was targeted". She held up a hand when Ben was about to speak.

"Why? ... At this moment we have no idea." She sighed. "It just so happened that it went down close to the farm. In a way, you're lucky we are here. Otherwise, God knows what would have happened had Calvin and I not found you."

Ben was getting a headache, he tried rubbing the tension from his neck and stopped. Looking up he said, "Wait... this makes no sense at all. If you found me earlier, why leave me there and why would someone target a plane; the plane that I was on?"

He watched them exchange a look. They were holding something back; he had to find out.

"Look, I know there is more than you're telling me. If it's something to do with me, I think I have a right to know."

Calvin raised his hands and backed away and looked at Sam. "This is your department."

"Don't remind me," she sighed, looking at Ben. "The FBI was informed two months ago, that there was a possible hit put on you."

Ben let out a bark of laughter. "Yeah, okay." When he saw the serious look on her face, the laughter turned to shock, then rage. "And I'm just finding this out now?"

Sam winced. "Well, yeah." She nodded. "We investigated it of course, but it was unfounded. Look, this may all just be a co-incidence. But the investigation needs to be opened again. For now, you're safe here with us. And as soon as we can get you out of here safely, we will. Now, do you know of any reason some-one would want you dead?"

Ben scratched his head. He was at a loss for words and so exhausted. "I haven't the faintest idea." Stifling a yawn, he cleared his throat. He didn't want to admit he had no real rec-ollection of his life other than Abbi. Sam, Daisy whatever her name was, had suspected it but to what extent, she didn't know, and he wasn't about to tell her either. "What I do know is that I need to get some sleep, preferably now."

"Here, I'll give you a hand," Calvin said, coming to Ben's aide. Holding his chair for him to stand up, Calvin jerked his head to the wall with the two doors. "The one on the right is the bathroom." Hurrying over to the other door, he shoved it wide. "And this one is the bedroom."

"Guide me to the bathroom, would you mate?" Ben puffed. He hated to admit it, but he had the strength of a newborn calf, all wobbly.

Calvin mumbled an apology. "Hang on, let me grab your crutches."

Ben waited and thought, *I need a plan. But first I need to take a piss then face plant on the bed and sleep for 12 hours.* Calvin came to him with the crutches in hand. Just as Ben went to take them, he felt his phone vibrate in his pocket. He paused.

Should I check it now? Something just didn't seem right about any of this. He couldn't pinpoint it, but something felt off.

Ignoring his phone, he hobbled his way to bathroom. Closing the door, he decided he'd wait until he was safely in the bedroom before checking it. He imagined that it was Abbi... Man he missed her. He needed to get out of this place and back to her, but knew it was best to wait for an ally. Maybe it was from lack of sleep but in his gut, he felt the two in the other room wasn't it. There was no way he could get far on his own.

Banging his way out of the bathroom, Ben looked to both agents. "Uh... I'm gonna head to bed," he said, jerking a thumb towards the closed door. "That is, if we're through here?"

Sam nodded. "Yeah, go ahead. We'll talk more in the morning. Have a goodnight."

"Thanks, you too." Ben nodded as he headed into the bedroom.

He closed the door behind him. By the light of the moon, he felt for a lock on the doorknob.

Damn there isn't one.

He glanced around the sparse room, looking for something, anything, he could push against the door. His glance fell to the spot beside him and saw a chair. Leaning one crutch against the wall, he took the chair and wedged it under the doorknob. He didn't trust either of them to not come in during the night. Hobbling over to the bed he dropped the other crutch with a bang. Flopping onto it, he pulled his cell out of his pocket and checked the notification.

There was a text from Abbi. Tears sprang to his eyes as he read it. She was close. God, he needed to hear her voice. Dialing her number, he waited for the call to connect.

"Ben?" He heard her say his name hesitantly, as if she wasn't sure, it was him.

"Hello, sweet one," he whispered. "I'm alone in a bedroom," he said, glancing around the moonlit room. "I can't say too much... just in case they are listening."

"Oh Ben, I was so worried," she sobbed. "I heard them take you, and you groaning in pain. What did they do to you? Where did they take you; do you know?" Her words tumbled out faster than he could respond.

"Abbi, hold up," he said gently. "I just wanted to tell you how much I miss you... how much I love you..." he trailed off. He could hear her crying. "Aww love, please don't. I didn't mean to make you cry." He felt horrible now, knowing he wasn't there to kiss her tears away.

"I love you, too," she said softly, weeping.

"There's something I need to tell you. I remember nothing, except you Abbi. I remember everything about us, about what we shared... but no one else." He sighed. "Not even my parents, how crazy is that?" he asked, not expecting an answer. "From what they told me, I'm an actor. A popular one apparently—"

"That's because you are an actor."

"Oh... Well, whatever happens, know that you are the best thing that has ever happened to me. That, I'm certain of..."

"I'm coming for you, Ben, so please don't think like that. You're coming home with me, and we are going to be home for Christmas. I don't care if I need to search every square inch of that forest your plane went down in. And God help the person who gets in my way," she said with fiery determination.

Despite her crying, he had to smile at the passion in her voice. When she set her mind to something, come hell or high water, nothing stopped her.

"Now, tell me all you can about where they took you," she urged.

"It's a short distance from where I was... no more than a kilometer I'd say, which direction, I have no idea. But. It seems to be a compound of sorts." He paused, trying to think of anything he could that would help her. "There's a dirt road that leads to the main building, it's white... and close to the road, actually. Oh, and it smells like skunks."

"Skunks? That's a bit strange, don't you think?"

"Well, that's because it's pot plants, Abbi..."

"Pot plants?" He could hear the growing confusion in her voice.

"Yes. It's an illegal grow op, in the middle of nowhere." He sighed. "And Abbi... they have guns."

"Guns?" She yelled it so loud he worried they heard her in the other room.

"Hush, Abbi! Yes, guns."

"Oh God, Ben." He could hear the panic rise in her voice. He hated to mention the guns, but he knew Abbi, if she could, she would find a way to him. She needed to be forewarned.

"Listen. I can't leave here on my own, at least not in this weather. There are two agents in the other room, one with the FBI and the other with the DEA. Now, this is important love. Take these names down and find out if they are who they claim to be."

"Claim to be?" She squawked.

"Yes, something isn't sitting well with me," Ben answered.

"Okay, I have a pen. What are their names?"

"Samantha Perkins, FBI and Calvin Falls, DEA. Do you think you can find out?" he asked.

"Yes, I'll get Tim to check them out for me. If they are who they say, then it shouldn't be a problem finding out."

That was a new name that came off her lips. "Tim? Uh... Who is Tim?"

"He's a cop, an old friend of mine. He pulled us over when I was speeding on the way down. He had some time off and is giving us a hand looking for you."

"You don't say..." Ben trailed off. Wondering just how close of a friend he was to come all this way.

Abbi must have caught the tone of his voice for she said, "Don't worry, Ben. He's just a friend. Wild horses couldn't drag me away from you..."

"I miss you woman," he murmured, tiredly.

"I miss you too. More than you'll ever know," she whispered.

They both heard the tell-tale beeping of a cellphone that was on its last charge. Ben knew it was his. He knew he shouldn't have called her, but he needed to hear her voice.

"Abbi, I need to go now."

"I know." Her voice broke. "I'm so sorry I didn't go with you when you wanted me to Ben. I should have gone."

"It's okay. I'm just happy it's me and not you. I wouldn't be able to cope as well as you, I'm afraid." He smiled. "I promise you, when this is all over and we are back home, I'm retiring." He could tell she was about to interrupt. "No, I'm serious Abbi if acting was so important to me, I'd remember it. I don't, I only remember you. So, I'm done with it, clearly, it's what got me into this predicament in the first place. And I don't ever want to leave you like this again."

She gave a tired chuckle. "I can't argue with you on that."

"Good," he murmured. He knew he should end the call, but he couldn't bring himself to do so. He wanted to hear her voice as he drifted off to sleep, to feel her satiny skin against his lips. He was torturing himself thinking of her like that. Needing to, he changed the subject.

"So, tell me. What do you want for Christmas?"

Not expecting the rapid topic change, Abbi laughed.

"You, Ben. I only want you..." she said, quietly.

Fighting to keep his eyes open, he said, "Abbi. I have no way to charge my phone, and I can't keep my eyes open. I need to go. Goodnight sweet one..." he murmured.

"Goodnight, I love you..." Her voice echoed through his mind as sleep overtook him.

Chapter 7

They were all sitting in the hotel cafe eating breakfast. Deciding to pass on the food, Abbi was on her fourth cup of coffee. She didn't trust her stomach for anything solid at that moment. Pulling a piece of paper from her pocket, she placed it on the table and slid it across to Tim. "Can you find out if these people are agents?"

"Sure thing." He nodded, stuffing a piece of toast in his mouth. Glancing down at the paper, he quickly looked up at her, a curious look in his eyes.

Abbi shivered. Rubbing her hands up and down her arms, she looked around for the source of a sudden draft. There wasn't one. Wrapping her hands around her mug, hoping its warmth would seep into her bones, she took a sip of her coffee then said, "Ben didn't really have a reason why he thinks they are lying. He just said something didn't sit right."

"No problem, I'll get right on it." He pushed away from the table. Taking out his cell, he walked a short distance away.

"Mark is expecting us to pick him up shortly. The doctor just discharged him." Ava leaned forward to look around Kim at her mother.

Abbi could see the concern etched on her face.

"Ah... mom. Do you want to come with us or stay here and get some rest?"

Seeing Kim was about to put her two cents into the conversation, Abbi held up her hand as she stifled a yawn.

"I'm coming." At their looks of worry, she added, "It's fine. Really, I'm fine. I got a few hours of sleep after I talked to Ben last night. Besides, Mark wants to get out to the site today and so do I." She wasn't fine, she was so utterly tired, but damned if she would admit it to them.

Kim pushed herself away from the table and stood. "Okay then. Let's go bust Mark out."

As they gathered their belongings, Tim returned to the table.

"Abbi, I made a call to a friend of mine. He's going to check those names out and get back asap." He grabbed a muffin and peeled the paper off then took a generous bite. "We ready to go, are we?" he asked, chewing around his words.

"Yeah, first stop is getting Mark. Then we gas up and head out to the crash site," Kim said, as they headed towards the exit.

They were silent as they walked to the rental. Abbi scowled at the sky. The sun was trying desperately to break through the heavy snow clouds. It was going to be hard enough to find where Ben had crashed. More of the white stuff would make it a hundred times worse.

"I'll drive," Tim said. "Who has the keys?"

Without a word, Abbi tossed him the fob and climbed into the back seat with Ava. She needed to close her eyes for ten minutes. A cat nap was all she needed.

ABBI JERKED WITH A start. Glancing around, she saw trees in every direction. Realizing she slept through picking up Mark at the hospital, she pulled her cellphone from her purse. Three hours had passed since leaving the hotel, and not a word from Ben. Yanking on the door handle, she shoved it open, and tumbled to the ground.

"Abbi, sweets! You're awake!" Mark came to her, helping her to stand. She closed the door leaning against the vehicle to get her bearings.

"Mark, I'm so sorry. I fell asleep."

Mark noticed the dark circles under her once bright eyes "Pfft... no worries. You needed the rest," he said, softly.

Nodding, she silently agreed as her eyes took in the sight before her. Trees that had been scorched by flames that had long died out, now stood broken and battered. Plane wreckage was all around them. The realization hit her like a ton of bricks. It was unbelievable that anyone walked away from that. *More than one person didn't walk away, Abbi...* She shook her head. She couldn't think of that right now. She had to focus what energy she had on finding Ben.

Unable to look away from the disaster before her, Abbi took a shaky breath and asked, "Mark... how far did you go before you stopped looking for Ben?"

He ran a hand through his hair. "I would say roughly a thousand feet in every direction."

She headed towards the driver's door of the SUV. "Okay. Tim?" she yelled. "Where are the keys?"

"In the ignition."

"Thanks." Abbi pulled the door open, jumping in behind the wheel, she said, "Mark, get in."

As she buckled her seat belt, she glanced at him. 'Which way was the plane coming from?" Raising her brows, she added, "And where was Ben sitting?"

"That way." Mark pointed as he pulled his seat belt around him. "And Ben had the window seat, towards the back of the plane. The one man that had passed away... uh... was sitting behind Ben. He was the last one I could find." He ducked his head and swiped his eyes on the sleeve of his coat.

Abbi reached over and gave his hand a squeeze.

"Okay. Hang on. It looks like it might get a bit bumpy," she said. Wanting to keep track of how far they went, Abbi hit the reset button of the trip counter on the dash.

Mark braced one hand on the dashboard and gripped the overhead bar with the other. He fought the panic that was gathering in his chest. She was right; it was damn bumpy. What made it worse was the fact that she was speeding down the middle of a forest. He refused to scream like a little girl going on her first roller coaster ride; despite wanting to. He chanced a glance at Abbi; she looked like she'd gone mad with her windswept hair and a crazed look in her eyes. *God, I hope she finds what she is looking for.*

Judging it to be a thousand feet, Abbi slowed down. Scanning every inch as they passed by, she looked for anything that might hold a clue. A piece of paper, wreckage from the plane... anything that would point to Ben being there.

"Does any of this look familiar?"

Mark shook his head. "No. Not really."

"What was he wearing?" She asked quietly.

"Jeans, boots, and a blue t-shirt." Mark chuckled.

"What?" Stopping the SUV, Abbi looked at him.

"He was also wearing that godawful yellow jacket you got him for his birthday." He flashed her an apologetic smile.

"He looks good in yellow. Besides, he likes it." She smiled at the memory of his excitement upon opening it. She raised a brow... In retrospect, he probably didn't like it so much, he'd been a little too excited over a jacket.

He nodded slowly. "Yeah... maybe."

"He's quitting Mark..." Abbi said softly.

"Come again?" Mark frowned, looking at her. "What are you talking about, Abbi?"

"Ben told me he's done. He's quitting acting... retiring... is what he said."

"No way! He can't just quit!" Mark spat out. "Every director in the industry wants him. He can't just do that. Think of the money he will lose!"

Abbi inhaled deeply. She removed her foot from the brake, letting the SUV coast. "Some things are more important than money. Besides, its his choice. I can't make that decision for him. He may change his mind. Speaking of which..." she paused. "Mark, he doesn't remember you or anyone else for that matter. Or that he's an actor. He only knows he is because the people that found him told him. All that he remembers is me..." She glanced at him. "He may never remember his past... And I'm not pressuring him to try."

Flabbergasted, Mark smacked his hand on his chest and stared at her with a horrified expression on his face. "He doesn't remember me! How could anyone not remember me?" He folded his arms across his chest and sulked. "I'm genuinely offended."

"I'm sure it will come back to him... in time," Abbi muttered absently, scanning the ground ahead. They had to of reached a thousand feet by now. Abbi glanced down at the trip counter and was shocked to see they had driven three miles. Looking up, she was about to tell Mark when her eye caught something ahead.

She felt her heart quicken its beat. It looked like broken trees. Not like the crash site where it was a gradual breakage. But trees that were snapped off at the base as if a truck had barreled through them.

She hit the gas and sped up just a tiny bit. Her heart felt like it would take flight as her eyes took in the scene. She pulled to a stop beside it as hope flared in her chest.

"Mark, come on. I think it's Ben's seat!" She jumped out of the vehicle not waiting for him.

Abbi knelt beside the abandoned snow-covered seat and put her hand on it. She was staring at it. Picturing Ben strapped to it, unconscious.

Wait a minute... this may not be his. But it *felt* like it was.

Tears sprang to her eyes as she glanced around, searching for anything that might belong to him.

Mark finally joined her and squatted. Nodding his head, he said, "Yup, that's his seat alright."

Abbi looked at him. "How can you be certain?" she asked in a hushed voice.

"You see this?" He pointed to a bit of red sticking out of a crease in the seat. Tugging on it, he pulled it free. Flipping it between his fingers, he stared at it and said, "Ever since meeting you, every time he flies, Ben sticks this in the seat he sits in." He held it out for her to take.

"What is it?" she asked.

"A note I suspect, but I have no idea, Abbi. He never did say, and I never asked."

She was afraid to see what Ben wrote. She imagined him thinking it may be the last thing he'd ever be able to say to her, Abbi hesitated before taking it.

She did. Slowly she unfolded the paper and read it. She promptly covered her face with her hands and burst into tears. The paper slipped from her fingers, fluttering to the ground.

Mark glanced at it... *'One moonlit night'*. His brow creased in thought. *What the hell...* "What does that even mean Abbi?"

She wiped her eyes with her sleeves and leaned back on her heels. "Ahh God. It means it is his seat. He was here." She ran her hand over it, stroking it as if it were Ben. Trying desperately to swallow her tears, she continued. "He once told me that he fell for me one moonlit night. The day we met," she said quietly, sniffling as the tears streamed down her face.

She took the note, carefully folded it, and put it in her bra over her heart for safekeeping. "Come on. We have to get back to the others." She hurriedly grabbed up anything she thought might belong to Ben. She didn't care if it was a button; she was taking it.

"You know what I don't get?" Mark asked.

"What's that?" She raised a brow.

"How could he not remember me? I mean, if it wasn't for me selling him my house..." He waved a hand in her direction. "He would never have met you."

Really? She turned towards the SUV and sighed. *He's still going on about that. I should never have told him.*

"I don't know Mark. The mind is a tricky thing. He didn't know me at first, either." Abbi glanced at him as she climbed behind the wheel, while Mark got in on the passenger side. "I'm sure it will all come back to him, it just takes time." She started the engine and put it into gear.

"Yeah. I guess you're right," he said, looking out the window as they drove back to the others.

"Mark, you know Ben loves you." It was easy for her to say, she knew. If the tables were turned, she would be having a much worse time of it than Mark.

"Yeah, I know." He motioned out the windshield and nodded towards the police cars parked up ahead. "Looks like the cavalry has arrived."

Abbi frowned as she pulled the vehicle to a stop then slowly got out.

"Abbi, Mark." Tim waved them over. "This is my friend I was telling you about. Sheriff Jack Martin."

Jack touched the brim of his hat and nodded. "Abbi, pleased to meet you." He stuck out his hand to Mark. "Mr. Donovan, I've heard a lot about you. I really admire your work."

Mark took the sheriff's hand in a firm grip. "Is that so? Call me Mark than." Glancing around, he waved at hand at the cop cars. "So, what brings you all out here?"

"Um... Mark, hold that thought," Tim said as he passed by him to walk to Abbi's side.

"Abbi, come with me, I have someone for you to meet." Tim took her by the arm and guided her towards an officer. "This is Deputy Marleen Chesterton. She has some questions she needs to ask."

Abbi glanced at Tim then at the officer. Something was up, and they didn't want her to know.

"Hi Abbi, how you are doing hunny?" Marleen smiled.

Abbi stared at her. Confidence oozed from every pore on her smiling face. Abbi wanted to dislike her for taking her away from what was going on but try as she might, she couldn't. She felt drawn to her.

Tired, Abbi sighed. "I'm doing okay."

"Oh, no you're not. Come here, girl." Marleen yanked open the front passenger door of her squad car. "You sit yourself down right there. Are you cold? Here let me get in the other side and I'll turn the heat on for you."

Abbi watched as she all but ran around the car to the driver side. "Wooeee, I gotta catch my breath! Here we go." Marleen smiled at Abbi as she cranked the heat.

Reaching into the back, Marleen grabbed a bag which she promptly shoved under Abbi's nose. "Do you want a cookie, hunny?"

Abbi chuckled, as she pushed the bag away. "Ah, no thanks."

Selecting one from within, Marleen stuffed it into her mouth. "You sure? They're chocolate mint."

Abbi held up a hand. "Positive. I'm good, thanks." Suspecting she needed some questions answered about Ben, Abbi glanced at her. "What was it you wanted to ask me?"

"Oh, right!" Marleen reached into the glove box in front of Abbi. "Oops," she giggled, catching the handgun that slipped. "Don't want that shooting off in here, now do we?"

Abbi's brows shot up. *Was this lady for real?* "Nope, we don't want that to happen." She chuckled and shook her head.

"Here we are!" Marleen held up a book triumphantly.

The Jasper Killings... She wants me to sign it...

"Would you mind?" Marleen raised hopeful eyes to her.

"Sure." Abbi felt her pockets. "Ah... I don't have a pen..."

Marleen smacked at hand to the pocket on her chest and pulled one out. "Here ya go." She clicked the end of it as she passed it to Abbi. With hope filled eyes, she looked at Abbi. "Can you sign it 'to my girlfriend Marleen'?"

Why the hell not? "No problem."

She signed the book and passed back the pen. Abbi held the book tightly to her chest. Something was bothering her; she just couldn't put her finger on it. Something about her book. She tried to remember it in detail. On any other given day, she could recite it word for word... well, mostly. But it was escaping her right now...

Squeezing the book tighter, Abbi looked at the woman beside her. "Marleen. Do you think I could look at this for a minute?"

The look Marleen gave her made Abbi feel like she thought she was a fraud. Like she didn't really write it. *Great... She thinks I'm some crazy lady who owns 20 cats...*

Holding the bag of cookies to her chest, Marleen stuffed another one in her mouth. Her eyes large in her round face. "Sure thing, hunny." She looked down at the bag that she held onto for dear life. Slowly she tilted it towards Abbi. "You want a cookie now?"

Abbi started to giggle; Marleen soon joined her. When the two looked at each other in the face they burst out laughing. As tears sprang to their eyes, Abbi nodded. "Yes, I'll take a cookie now."

She smiled her thanks. As she reached into the bag, both looked out the window and noticed the others looking at them as if they were nuts. Which promptly had them laughing hysterically. It felt good to let off a little tension, even if was over something as silly as a damn cookie. That was until she saw the look on Mark's face...

Chapter 8

"Wait, what?" Mark raised his brows in outrage. "Whoa, whoa, whoa." He motioned for a timeout. "Let me get this straight..." He stood a moment, looking up at the trees as he rubbed his jaw. Finally, he looked at the sheriff. "What do you mean, they *aren't* agents? Then who the hell are they?"

"We aren't entirely sure," Jack said.

Mark stepped closer and raised his brows. Fearing that Abbi would overhear, in a hushed tone he asked, "Hadn't you better find out?"

Tim put out a hand, urging Mark to stay put. "These things take time, Mark. We can't just go in there with guns blazing. Ben could be killed... if it's who we think it is."

"Yeah, well Abbi isn't going to wait. She'll flip," Mark said, looking worriedly at the squad car she was currently sitting in. The laughter coming from within carried to him and the officers. Mark saw the exact moment when she realized something was terribly wrong.

Mark nodded. *Yup. Here it comes now.* He watched as she came flying out of the car and rushed over to them as she stuffed something into her coat pocket.

Tears in her eyes she looked at then men standing there. "What is it?" Willing the cookie, she just ate to stay down she clenched her teeth. Hoping beyond hope that she wouldn't

77

lose it all over someone's shoes. "Someone better tell me what the hell is going on!"

She looked at Tim, watching him as he wiped his hand over his mouth then cleared his throat.

"Uh... Abbi. Ben was right. Those people aren't agents..."

She lowered her head and watched as the tip of her boot dug into the blackened earth. Tears spilled over her lashes, blinding her, yet she still gazed at the ground.

"Abbi, sweets. Are you okay?" Mark asked, gently.

Her head bobbed up and down rapidly. She was going to lose it; she could feel it. Slowly she started to shake it from side to side as a low keening of agony escaped past her quivering lips.

"Come here." Mark enfolded her into his arms, holding her as she sobbed.

The one thing that kept her going was thinking that Ben was safe with the agents. How foolish she was. Abbi pulled away from Mark. She needed answers now.

"Sheriff, do you have any clue who they might be?" she asked, wiping her coat sleeve across her face. She noted the glance cross between Sheriff Martin and Tim, one she didn't like.

"Abbi..."

With one look Abbi effectively cut off Tim from finishing.

"Sheriff?" One brow arched in his direction; Abbi waited. The longer he took, the madder she got. "Are you going to answer my question?"

"We aren't sure who they are..."

"Bullshit! You know very well who they are, so stop stalling and tell me."

Sheriff Jack Martin sighed. "I'm not at the liberty to discuss this with you, it's an open investigation."

Looking around in wonder, Abbi smacked her thigh in frustration. "Right. An open investigation. I should have guessed." With contempt, she whipped around, and stalked towards the vehicle.

"Abbi, where are you going now?" Tim called.

"Back to the hotel and if none of you want to walk, you best get in." She slammed the driver's door and revved the engine to life.

Ava looked at Kim and Mark. "Oh Lord, she's not kidding." All three scrambled to get to the SUV before she tore out of there.

"Tim, you better haul ass if you're coming with us," Mark called.

"I'm coming!" Tim hurtled over a fallen tree and ran. Diving into the back seat, he tucked is feet in and slammed the door as the SUV was thrown in reverse.

Abbi spun the vehicle around and hit the gas.

"Jesus Abbi! Are you trying to scare the shit outta me?" Tim yelled.

Mark looked at him from the front seat as he once again gripped the bar.

"Buddy, you better hang on," he muttered, turning his head back to look out the windshield.

Breathing quickly, Kim yelled, "Abbi for cripes sake slow down!" She hated going faster than a snail's pace. Kim covered her face when she saw that Abbi had no intention of stopping where the forest met the highway.

"Mom, you need to slow down, now!" Ava demanded.

As she cranked the wheel hard to the right, the tires squealed onto the pavement, Abbi realized she had enough. Stomping on the brakes, the SUV came to a screeching halt. Abbi sat there and gripped the steering wheel.

Slowly she turned in her seat and was met with four sets of terrified eyes staring back at her. She wanted to scream at them all to shut the hell up but counted to ten instead.

"I'm sorry," she mumbled, mentally cursing at each one. "I..." she smoothed her hair down. "I had a moment. It won't happen again." She turned back in her seat and continued to drive south.

Tim gave Ava a look. Silently he mouthed to her, 'Where is she going?'

Ava frowned and squinted, shaking her head, she silently conveyed she didn't understand.

He leaned forward and did the same thing to Kim. She raised her brows and asked, "What the hell are you trying to say?"

Tim cleared his throat. "I said where is she going?"

The others remained silent, knowing now was not the time to ask Abbi anything.

Abbi raised her eyes to the rear-view mirror. She looked back at the road.

Where am *I going?*

The hotel was in the opposite direction. She had every intention of going that way, but something was tugging her south and damned if she would deny it.

After twenty minutes on the road, Abbi stuck her arm out in front of Mark. "Pull," she said, then glanced at him. The look on his face, one would think she had thrown a slug at him.

He was shocked that she broke the silence. "*What?*"

She shook her arm. "My sleeve... pull on it will you? I'm hot."

Mark nodded. Not saying a word, he tugged on her sleeve as she pulled her arm free.

Abbi smiled her thanks.

"Do you want me to drive Abbi?" he offered.

"Nope."

He looked out his window, watching... for what he didn't know. "Okay... it was just a thought." Mark glanced back at her. "Ah, Abbi. Where *are* you going?"

"I'll know when we get there."

He let out a shaky laugh. "Of course, you will." He glanced at the others; his laughter turned mechanical. "Why didn't we think of that?"

THE SUV ATE MILE AFTER mile along the lonely, paved road. The sun was rapidly making its decent on another day. Up ahead there was a town according to the road sign. Martinsville, population 5000. Abbi fleetingly wondered if it was named after the Sheriff's family. She didn't like Jack Martin. She had no clue why, but for some reason he rubbed her the wrong way. Maybe because she was so damned tired. Tired of driving, tired of crying and especially tired of missing Ben.

Before she knew it the sun was down, and the odd tear still slipped down her cheek as the streetlights streamed in the darkened car. She would never forgive herself if something happened to him. He was her light in a dark and cold world. Abbi felt a hand cover hers on the gearshift. She looked down to see Mark's hand on hers.

"Abbi. I think it's time we pulled over for the night, okay?"

She pulled her hand away, and quickly swiped her cheeks. She nodded in agreement.

"Mom, there's a bed-and-breakfast." The tiredness clear in her voice, Ava pointed. "Why don't we stop there for the night."

Abbi took a deep breath, wanting desperately to sound like she was in control. She failed miserably at it. Instead, it came out as a mumble. "Sure, that sounds great."

She signaled and pulled the SUV into the driveway. There before them stood an old Victorian home on a corner lot. Something that looked like it could be home to a vampire.

"Um, guys... you sure about this?" Kim squeaked, as she peered up at the house from her window.

"Hell yes!" Tim smacked his hands together. "Now this is the perfect spot for a movie, huh, Mark?"

Mark glanced out the window. "Sure... for a horror movie."

Ava yawned. "I don't care if it's haunted. I'm so tired it won't make a bit of difference."

"Nothing can be as scary as Abbi's driving." Kim grinned at her sister.

"You're alive, aren't you?"

She loved her sister dearly but watching the grin fall from Kim's face put a spring to Abbi's step.

Ava pushed past everyone taking the steps two at a time. "Come on. Let's check in." As she raised her hand to knock, the door swung open.

There before them stood a little old lady. A smile beaming on her wrinkled face.

Looking Abbi in straight in the eye, she held out her hand. "Abbi... We have been expecting you. Welcome to our humble abode. You all must be exhausted from that long drive. My name is Hester Riley."

All five of them looked from one to the other. The same question mirrored in their eyes... How did she know they had been driving for so long and how the hell did she know Abbi by name... and who was the 'we' that was expecting them?

Chapter 9

B en could feel Abbi's warm breath on his face as he gazed into her eyes. God he would never tire looking into those orbs. She smiled at him.

"I've missed you my love," he murmured as he tucked a silky strand of hair behind her ear. He tilted her chin upward with his finger and slowly bent to touch his lips to her soft mouth. The thrill had him groaning from the pain in his leg.

Instantly awake, Ben bolted upright in bed. Grimacing as he glanced around, searching for Abbi. He found himself alone in the darkened room. It was all just a dream.

His gaze darted to the door. The chair was still propped under the knob, just as it had been every night since he had arrived in this hell hole.

Feeling defeated he searched the bed for his phone. He thumbed the power button on. He had sent Abbi a quick text before shutting it off, to tell her he was doing so. It was the only way to save what little battery life it had left. Thankfully, it held onto its charge. If he used it sparingly it might just last.

When was that again? A day ago, two? Waiting for the home screen to load before checking to see when he sent it, he hoped that she responded. But the shrilling of a phone startled him. Fumbling he caught it just before it hit the floor. Flipping it over in his hand, he realized the ringing came from the other room. Holding his breath, he listened to see if anyone would answer. Sam's 'hello' came through the thin walls of the cabin.

Scooting to the edge of the bed, he silently grabbed the crutch from the floor.

Who would be calling her at 2:00 am?

He hobbled as quietly as he could to the door. Panting from the excursion, he placed his ear against it, and strained to listen.

"Of course, boss...Yes, it was me that brought the plane down just as you requested."

What in the actual hell...?

Sam paused. Listening to the caller, Ben imagined. Her next words had him cocking his head.

"Mr. Everett? Ah yes. The passenger's name record indicated he was on the flight."

Who is she talking about? He moved his head and flattened his ear against the crack in the door. He dared not take a breath.

"No sir. There is no sign of him at this moment. After seeing the wreckage firsthand as you well know, I can guarantee he was killed in the crash, it will be weeks before his body is found, I'm sure... Why thank you sir! Yes, I hope the client is thrilled as well.... I'm always available if you're needing... shall we say, 'another hit'.

Ben backed away in horror. He'd known something was off, but this? He slowly made his way back to the bed. He needed to think, to make sense of all this in his muddled mind. Something was way off. That was a definite, yes... he just couldn't put his finger on it.

Now what the hell am I going to do? Sam obviously is the 'hit-man'...does that mean Smitty is too? And who the bloody hell is Mr. Everett? He got up and stumbled to the window. He had to come up with a plan.

Glancing out the frosty edged pane of glass, he saw that it had stopped snowing. The snow swirled along the ground, drifting here and there. He leaned on the sill, searching for anything that could be a landmark he could tell Abbi about. There was nothing but the road and mile after mile of bare trees.

He thought he saw the twinkling of lights through the trees. If that were the case, maybe there was a house or a town nearby. He needed to get outside. The cabin was one floor so it wouldn't be that bad of a fall if he climbed out the window. Relief filled him as he looked at the ground. He could just crawl over the ledge and stand on the ground. Gripping the handles, he lifted the sash an inch. The cool breeze hit him like a blast from a freezer.

Wait... you need to tell Abbi first.

He softly closed it. As much as he wanted to leave, he knew if he took off now without anyone knowing he had left, he'd freeze to death before he was found.

Ben sighed heavily as he turned back to the bed and sat down. He had to figure this out. Rubbing his forehead in thought, he set out to do just that.

Why was Smitty so helpful if he was in on this? At least he acted helpful.

Something about this was all so damn familiar, he couldn't shake that feeling for the life of him. He laid back, willing his mind to remember what it was. Vague images as if he were walking in fog flashed through his mind. Frustration overtook him. It was no use, the harder he tried to remember the worse the pictures in his mind clouded over. He would need to relax and not think so hard.

A bang in the room next to his, startled him upright. Someone had flung the outside door open.

"Dean what the hell?" Sam hissed.

Does that woman not sleep?

It was a damn good thing he hadn't left. He never would have gotten far if he had. He was sure that man would love any excuse to put a bullet in his head.

"Where is he?" Dean slurred.

"Who? Smitty?" Sam asked.

"Smitty's on watch. No. Mr. Hollywood."

Ben could hear the legs of a chair being dragged, then a thud. Dean must have sat down.

"You know full well I have to keep an eye on him. He's sleeping in the bedroom." Sam said, in hushed tone. "Or he was until you came barging in..."

"I know what you're up to old woman..."

Old woman? Sam must be in character

"Is that so? And what might that be?"

By that time, Ben was back standing at the door. Carefully he eased the chair from under the doorknob. Despite her trying to kill him, he knew if things got ugly between the two, he would have to intervene. He reached for the doorknob and slowly turned it.

"You're trying to cash in on him. You're going to call the cops any day now and demand a ransom... I want in on it," Dean said with wickedness.

Ben's hand froze.

"Is that so? How much?" Sam questioned.

Piss on that... Ben grabbed the chair, stuck it back under the doorknob and made his way to the bed. *What the hell was I thinking...* he wondered sitting down.

For some reason he hadn't been. If someone had talked to Abbi like that, they would not be standing for long. But Sam wasn't Abbi. Not even close. He clearly didn't think, he just acted. A mistake he wouldn't make again.

Laying down on the bed, his thoughts turned to the woman he loved. Where they had been, since discovering his cellphone clenched tightly in his hand; strapped to a seat in the middle of the forest.

His phone lit up the room. Picking it up, he hit the text notification. His face softened when he saw her name.

'I know you're likely sleeping Ben, and that you won't get this till after we find you, but I had to tell you. We found where your seat landed... and I have your note. I never told you this, but I fell in love with you the same moonlit night on my front porch. I never wanted to let you go then and I still don't now. I just thought you should know that. Love Abbi'

He wanted so badly to respond. But he couldn't. He knew if he did, what little charge he had left would quickly be depleted. He pressed the power button, as one single tear ran down his cheek...

Ben awoke to sunlight streaming through the window and a dire need to use the bathroom. Feeling as weak as a newborn, he struggled to sit up. Leaning over the edge of the bed, he picked up his crutches and moved to stand. A wave of dizziness had him almost toppling backwards onto the bed. He had to get out of there, today. He didn't care if he died trying. It would be better than being locked up in this hell hole a minute longer.

He'd already worked out the plan in his head. He would go out to the other room where Sam aka Daisy would be having her morning coffee and smoke. They would make small talk like they did for the past few days, and then she would leave to go work at the farm across the yard. He would be left alone for the next few hours until someone came to check on him. That time in between is when he would make his escape. But first, he would let Abbi know his intentions. Hopefully, she would get to him in time. Before someone showed up, most likely Smitty.

There was something about that man that was not adding up. He wasn't cold like Sam. To put it bluntly she was a certified bitch. Smitty genuinely seemed concerned about him. Bringing him food and pain meds, along with the daily newspaper. No, Smitty wasn't anything like the others.

Ben made his way to the door. He removed the chair, like he did every morning since getting there from underneath the doorknob. Opening the door, he mumbled, "Good morning." Then headed to the bathroom.

He was washing his hands when he happened to look at his reflection in the mirror above the sink. He stopped. Staring at the stranger before him. He was stunned, realizing he hadn't seen his reflection since the accident. He must have lost weight as his eyes seemed sunken. He looked down at his clothes. They were a bit loose, and stained, wreaking of sweat and blood. He glanced back up at the mirror. A beard hid the gauntness of his face and the pallid skin beneath. He was confident that he'd never had a beard in his life. Judging from the photos on his phone at least. Either way, it would have to go, it itched like he had been bitten by fleas. Which didn't surprise him any if that were the case, considering his current living conditions.

He opened the cabinet and looked for a pair of scissors and razor. As he did, he heard the outside door slam shut followed by footsteps across the wood plank floor. The sound of a chair being dragged from under the table, told him exactly who it was. Dean...

The beard would have to wait. Ben reached out and turned the doorknob. Taking a steadying breath, he pulled the door open. The two sitting at the table watched as he made his way over. He pulled out a chair and sat down hard.

Glancing towards Sam, he saw her in character as Daisy. It was on the tip of his tongue to comment on that fact in front of Dean but thought better of it. He didn't know what shit storm that would create. Instead, he turned and stared at Dean with hatred.

"What's your problem?" Dean sneered.

Ben squinted.

"I'll tell you what my problem is. Or better yet. I can show you. Give me a baseball bat and let me smash your leg with it and maybe then you'll see what my problem is, hmm?"

Dean snickered in response. He pointed at Ben. "I like you. It just so happens today is your lucky day I'd say."

At Daisy's questioning look, Dean sent her conspiratorial wink.

"You get to meet the boss man of this here operation. He'll decide your fate."

Daisy made a sound in her throat.

Dean sent her a warning look. "Hush old woman. The boss requested an audience with Mr. Hollywood." He pushed away from the table and came around to Ben. "Come on. It's show-time. Move it, let's go."

Ben got up from the table. *Well, there goes my plans of escaping... for now.*

He followed Dean from the cabin with Daisy, shuffling along to bring up the rear. Ben had to give her credit; she was a convincing actress...

Actress? Hmm. Now that makes sense...

Brightness from the sun assaulted Ben's eyes causing him to fumble on a rock. Dean caught him just in time before he fell to the ground. In a low whisper that only Ben could hear, Dean said, "It's okay buddy. I got you."

Ben stared at him in shock. What happened to the badass from moments before? He had to be imagining it.

"This way lady and gent," Dean boomed as he opened the door to the farm. The smell of so many marijuana plants, hit Ben like a brick wall.

Something was making him feel sick. He swallowed trying to stop the nauseous bile from surging up his throat. Yes, the scent was over-whelming, but Ben knew it wasn't that. It was the fact that in his weakened state anyone wanting to do a little practice shooting could easily use him as target.

The trio trudged on, towards the back of the building Dean led them to a door. Pushing it open, he stepped aside allowing Ben to enter first.

Ben glanced around the room; his eyes fell at once on the man standing against the wall. Smitty. He looked as if he was the one that was facing the firing squad.

The room smelled of stale cigar smoke and brandy. Two plush leather chairs were placed in front of a large mahogany desk that sat in front of a bay window overlooked a river. The chair slowly swiveled around. Ben felt relief when he saw who the man was sitting behind the desk.

Wait...Dean called him the boss man... This just keeps getting better and better...

The man leaned forward and offered his hand to shake.

"Well hello Mr. Everett. It's nice to finally meet you." He gestured to one of the chairs. "Take a load off."

Ben ignored the proffered hand and sat, baffled at being called by the name of Everett again.

Chapter 10

"Okay then." Sheriff Jack Martin said, leaning back in his chair. He picked up a sheet of paper that was laying on his desk and scanned it. His brows drew together in a frown as he laid the paper on the desk and folded his hands in front of him.

Ben Everett had quite the lengthy career record.

Jack glanced at him sitting there across the desk. His clothes were dirty and disheveled. The smell of his stench reached his nostrils clear across the desk. Jack Martin wrinkled his nose in distaste. He wondered what the big shot actor thought about his current predicament.

"So, Ben. You don't mind me calling you by your given name now do you son?"

"Would it matter. No?" Ben shook his head. "I didn't think so."

Jack nodded. He pointed to the paper on his desk. "I got my boys to do a little digging. Seeing how in these parts, most have never heard of you. You're quite the star, aren't you?"

Ben couldn't confirm nor deny what he said. That part of his memory was still missing, he shrugged his shoulders in way of an answer.

"It also says that you are living in Canada with Abbi Petersen. Now, that name folks around here know of. I already knew that, having the pleasure of meeting the little hell cat myself," he said.

When a lecherous smile spread on his fat greasy lips, Ben had to restrain himself from flying across the desk to throttle the man. Instead, he took a deep breath, with nostrils flared he shot the Sheriff a deadpan stare. "Do you have a point to all this interrogation sheriff?"

"I do. I think we will keep you just a bit longer. I'll give Abbi a call. Anonymously of course. Telling her that if she wants to see you alive again, she'll pay up. Perhaps...in more ways than one."

Ben gripped the arms of his chair, resisting the urge to beat the smile off that fat smug face. He wasn't surprised in the least to hear about a ransom. How many times was that now? Too many to count. But for him to talk about Abbi like that was more than he could take and the sooner he got out of there the better. There wasn't a doubt in Ben's mind that if he threw a punch the hired thugs would be all over him before he could make contact.

Ben sent the man a murderous stare. "Are we through here?" That was all he had to say to see the instant fear spring to the Sheriffs face.

Jack nodded rapidly. "Certainly. You can go back to the cabin now."

Satisfied, Ben inclined his head as if he were dismissing the man.

Heaving himself up from the chair, he slowly made his way to the door. Turning back, he gave one last long look before exiting. Stepping out into the hall with Daisy and Smitty right behind him, he heard the Sheriff talking to Dean. His words almost caused Ben to falter, but he refused to show any emotion. Because come dawn, Dean was ordered to send him to his maker.

They turned down the hallway that led to the clinic and the door to outside. "I'll take him back to the cabin Daisy," Smitty said

"Sure, I have some paperwork to go over." She sounded relieved, as she scurried towards her office.

"Come on Ben, I'll get you something to eat." Smitty held the door for him to cross the threshold to outside.

The sun was no longer blinding as clouds gathered in the sky. It had the look and feel of snow in the air, but Ben didn't care, he'd made up his mind; he was leaving tonight one way or another.

Neither man said a word, both lost in their thoughts as they made their way to the cabin.

Smitty hurried ahead to open the cabin door for Ben. Once inside, he went right to the table and collapsed on the closest chair.

"What do you feel like eating?" Smitty asked.

All Ben wanted to do was sleep right in the chair. He didn't even have the energy to fall into the bed. "Nothing, I'm not hungry."

Smitty opened the fridge and took out a carton of eggs. Slapping a frying pan on the stove he turned the element on high and quickly cracked six eggs in the sizzling pan. Whipping them with a fork, he said, "You need to eat, you have to keep your strength up."

Ben wasn't giving his intentions away. There was no way he would even hint that he was planning an escape.

"For what, just to be killed at dawn?" He spat out.

Smitty turned from the stove to look at him.

"Were you not listening the first night you came here?" Smitty asked.

Ben squinted in thought and shook his head. His stomach growled at the smell coming from the stove. He leaned back in his chair trying to appear relaxed and laid his hands on the rumbling, hoping to silence it.

Here it is the part about him being with the DEA...

"Right..." Ben nodded, "You and Sam being agents." He folded his arms across his chest. He didn't buy their story then and he wasn't now. Sam made it perfectly clear what kind of agent she was.

Smitty turned the stove off and dumped the eggs onto a plate. Sitting it before Ben he said, "Yeah that's it. I talked to my superior and I was given the order to take you out."

"Come again?" Ben asked.

Just how many people have it in for me?

"Hell. No! I didn't mean 'take you out' as in shoot to kill. I meant remove you from here!"

Ben let his guard down, just a bit. A tiny sliver of hope flared in his chest.

"When?" He asked, picking up the fork he dug into the eggs.

Smitty brought two cups of steaming coffee to the table. Sitting down, he leaned towards Ben.

"Tomorrow morning, at 4 am." Smitty pointed to the plate. "You might want to slow down on that just a bit. You might get sick."

Ben's hand froze midway to his gaping mouth. He looked down at the eggs.

Did Smitty poison them? No. I need to trust someone.

Shrugging, he stuck the fork in his mouth and looked at Smitty. "Why so late?"

If this fails, at dawn I'm a goner.

"Dean is on the night watch tonight. He always falls asleep around 3:30. By 4 am he will be well off to lala land."

Ben nodded. Stuffing the last of the eggs in his mouth, he savored the last bite.

He pushed the plate away then picked up his coffee mug and took a sip. "So. What's the plan?"

"The plan is simple. You crawl out of your window at exactly 4:00 am. I'll keep watch from across the clearing to make sure you're not spotted. Sit tight for a minute. If it's all clear, I'll send out three sharp whistles. There will be a van waiting down the road a bit. You will have to walk though. Do you think you can manage?"

Ben nodded. If it meant getting out of this hell hole and back to Abbi, he'd crawl if he had to.

"Good, you better get some rest." Smitty looked at his watch. "You have 16 hours."

Ben chuckled. "I'm sure I'll be well rested by then." He frowned. Should he mention what he'd overheard Sam and Dean talking about the other night?

Thinking it for the best he took a deep breath. "Ah, can I mention one thing that's been bugging me?"

"Shoot."

"The other night Dean came bursting in at around 2 am. He said he knew what Sam was up to. Though he called her Daisy." Ben looked at Smitty for a reaction. There was none.

"Yeah? Well, he only knows her as Daisy. Go on."

"He wanted to split on the ransom he knew she was going to ask for me. If she's an agent, she's a dirty one."

Smitty nodded. "I had my doubts about her too." He took a sip of his coffee. "We arrived together, as joint investigators. At once I felt something off and so I contacted my superior over it. There is an 'agent' Sam Perkins and by that, I mean her undercover name. We never use our real names when under-cover." He paused. He had the look of a person that had giv-en too much information out. He shrugged and continued. "I can't vouch for her as a person. Being from different agencies, I never knew her before. I shouldn't have told you all of that, but I'm trying to be as transparent as much as possible."

Ben nodded. "I really appreciate it mate." He frowned. Something was still bothering him, and he had to ask. "So how long have you two been here?"

"Four months, one month longer than Dean."

"Dean? I thought he would have been here longer, given his role. He's what? The manager?" Ben asked nonchalantly.

Smitty chuckled. "He likes to think he is. I had him checked out too. He has a criminal record longer than your arm."

Ben nodded and scratched his beard. "Bloody hell, this thing is driving me nuts."

"Hey. Do you want a shower? I can get you a razor and a change of clothes?"

"I would give up my left nut for one." Ben laughed.

"No need for that." Smitty raised his hand and got up from the table. "I'll be right back. If you want, get in now and I'll leave everything on that table there by the bathroom." He walked to the door and stopped. Turning around to look at Ben, Smitty said, "I know this really isn't the time to ask. But when this is all said and done, can I get your autograph?"

Ben smiled genuinely for the first time in what felt like months.

"I'll do one better than that. If you get me out of here alive and back to Abbi in one piece, I'll fly you up to Canada for a week."

"Right on!" Smitty laughed, as he headed out the door.

BEN LAID STARING AT the ceiling. Darkness had fallen some time ago judging by the light of the full moon. He had no idea what the time was, but it felt like it was past midnight. Surprisingly, he had slept most of the day. A good solid eight hours, or at least his body felt like he had. He hadn't felt this energized in God knew how long. A hot shower and a shave would do that to anyone. But that wasn't it. He knew it was the thought of seeing Abbi again that had him feeling this way.

Despite being well rested, he felt himself drifting off to sleep again. That was until he heard Abbi crying the name Franklin in his ear. He bolted upright in bed. His eyes drawn to a faint misty apparition in the corner by the door. He rubbed them, sure that what he was seeing was nothing more than the light of the moon shining through the trees. It wasn't...it was still there.

"Hello?" He said in a hushed whisper.

A young man stared at him from the corner. Dressed in an old army uniform, he floated towards the bed in a misty haze, stopping beside it, he pointed towards the window.

Ben heard the man's voice, not out loud, but in his mind, telling him it was time to go.

Within a second the figure of the young man disappeared into a misty fog as it passed through the glass pane of the window.

He shook his head.

It was just a dream Ben. Nothing more than a dream...But if it really was a dream...why am I sitting up wide awake?

God, he needed a splash of cold water on his face.

Trying to put it all behind him, he felt for his phone. Without picking it up he pressed the power button, needing to know the time.

Surprised at how chilly the room was he grabbed his coat from the foot of the bed and tugged it on. Picking up his phone he turned it over. The display lit up the room, a chill ran up his spine... it was 3:55 am. He had five minutes before he was to climb out the window.

Seeing that he had a missed text from Abbi, he quickly opened it. A soft smile came to his lips. A simple 'Hi' was all it said. Man, he missed her. He started to send her a reply letting her know what was going on, but had a last second thought, he would send it to all the people she had mentioned before. Adding Mark, Ava, and Kim from his contacts to the message, his thumb paused over the send button.

No... I better wait.

He didn't want to jump the gun in case he never made it outside. He didn't want Abbi anywhere near here if it could be helped. Especially if he got caught.

The battery, with any luck with hold its charge. At twenty percent, he was confident he would be able to send it later. Lucky for him, he'd been able to sneak using Daisy's charging cord when she was gone.

He saved it as a draft and shoved it in his pocket. As soon as he was outside, he would send it. Taking a deep breath, he gripped the handles on the window sash. Slowly inch by inch he raised it. Unexpectedly a loud creak echoed in the room.

"Sonofabitch!" He was kicking himself for not cracking it open earlier when he had been alone in the cabin. He waited for the telltale footsteps that would tell him that someone heard.

Nothing. He shoved it open all the way. His breath hitched in his throat as a blast of cold air rushed in. Leaning out he looked around. There was a corner to the right of the window that was in shadows. The perfect spot to wait.

Now to act. But how? He looked down at the crutches, deciding the best choice was to put one crutch out the window followed by his good leg. He set out to do just that. Slowly he maneuvered outside. Panting, from the exertion, he leaned back in the corner and glanced around. Satisfied he was alone he took his phone from his pocket. Looking down, he hit the send button on the message just as he heard the unmistakable slide of a 40 caliber semi-automatic being cocked.

"Did you honestly think I was going to let you get away?" Daisy motioned with the gun. "Come on, move it."

Where the hell is Smitty?

Feeling defeated, Ben slowly moved from the corner. Rounding the side of the cabin he headed towards the front. The sound of a shotgun being cocked echoed in the stillness.

"Not so fast there, little lady."

Ben stopped and turned around at the unmistakable sneer. Dean stood, pointing a gun at Daisy's head.

Bloody hell! This just keeps getting better and better...

Chapter 11

Abbi was laying on an ancient settee in the sitting room of the old B&B, while Mark sat in an armchair by the fireplace. She could already feel the kink starting in her neck as her head leaned uncomfortably on the wooden arm. She needed to get up but couldn't bring herself to move.

She waited, phone in hand, willing Ben to respond. It was silly she knew, but she had just sent him a text; a simple 'Hi'. He never did respond to her last one, the one telling him when she fell in love with him. She doubted he would be up at 3:30 am, yet she remained still.

A few minutes longer wouldn't hurt. She was foolish she knew. Days ago, he'd told her his phone was dying. There was no way it held its charge.

She had long ago stopped listening to Mark prattle on about how Ben really should rethink his retirement. Sitting before the cozy fireplace in Hester Riley's parlor, they had been discussing how strange it was that they hadn't been kept in the loop to the progress of the investigation. What was even stranger, was the fact that everyone seemed to stop talking about the plane crash and the fact that Ben was still missing.

"Abbi? ... Abbi, are you asleep?" Mark asked in a loud whisper.

She looked at him. "No."

He raised his brows in question. "Did you not hear a word I said?"

"Um... No?"

At his frown, she felt the need to apologize. "I'm sorry Mark, my mind is not in the present. It has nothing to do with you, I promise. It's just—"

"Ben. I know, I get it."

"Yeah," she replied, softly.

A sudden overwhelming sadness came over her, one that made her wonder if it would ever go away. She shook her head, not wanting to think about it and said, "What was it you were saying?"

"Oh nothing."

Nodding, she glanced back down at her phone.

"I just wondered what it was you stuffed in your pocket."

She wrinkled her brow. "What? When?"

"The other day when you came flying out of the cop's cruiser."

She slowly sat up. She had no recollection of it.

What was it she had stuffed in there?

"Where is my coat?" She sat her cellphone on the table and stood.

"Ava hung it on the coat tree in the foyer." Mark nodded towards the general direction of it.

He watched as she sailed out of the room only to return a minute later with the coat in her hands. She pulled the pockets out. A balled-up tissue, some loose change, and a gum wrapper spilled onto the coffee table beside her cellphone.

Mark shook his head as he looked at the table. "Nope, none of that." He spread his hands apart. "It was something fairly large."

"Which pocket was it?" Abbi looked at him for the answer.

"The right inside pocket, Abbi. I watched you put it in when you flew out of the car."

She fumbled, turning the coat to face her. Sticking her hand in she pulled out a copy of the Jasper Killings.

Her book! Now she remembered. She'd asked Marleen if she could look at it. She must have absently stuck in in her pocket in her hurried state.

"Huh," Mark said. "Do you always carry that around?"

"Of course not. Its Marleen's." Abbi glanced at him and noticed the confusion on his face.

"The cop. You know, the female one who had me sit in her car while you were talking to the sheriff and Tim."

"Oh, that's right! Why do you have it?"

"I asked her if I could look at it for a minute." She sat down on the couch, cross legged and hugged it to her chest.

"Ah, okay...Why? You wrote it."

Abbi flipped through the pages, she was in the middle of searching for something, she wasn't sure what it was. "I'll know when I find it..."

With a worried look on his face Mark's eyes grew large as he nodded. "Rigghht."

He got up and laid a hand on her shoulder. "I'm going to bed Abbi. Don't stay up too late." He gave her a brotherly kiss on the top of her head and walked towards the stairs. Stopping at the archway, he paused and looked back at her.

He was worried of the uncertainty of Ben's disappearance, but he was also worried about Abbi. Not only was his best friend missing but he was afraid Abbi was losing her mind. He just wasn't sure which was worse...

Abbi suddenly felt cold. She put her coat on and stuffed her belongings, where they belonged back in her coat pockets. She checked her cell to see if Ben had replied, it was 3:46 am. Disappointed that he hadn't, she dropped it in her pocket too. Sitting on the edge of the settee, she opened her book and scanned through the chapters.

"Here it is," she mumbled to herself.

Detective Ethan Fields surveyed the scene before him. The day that changed hundreds of lives forever. This was no 'accident'. No. This was a crime. A cold-hearted, premeditated crime.

Passenger trains did not just blow up while travelling on the rails across the countryside. Ethan glanced around. And they sure as hell didn't blow asteroid sized holes in the ground either.

The gaping hole in the earth only confirmed his suspicions. No. Someone was after Kingston Parker the Third. Heir to a mighty fortune...in paper products of all things. He was to be on that train. There was no way that someone would wake up one morning and decide today was the day. The day to blow up a train full of strangers. But who would do such a thing, Ethan wondered?

The most logical place to look first was the family. But Kingston Parker was the only living heir and the last in his family lineage. No, it had to be someone with a grudge...

Abbi snapped the book shut. She leaned back, slowly exhaling, staring off into space.

Was there a connection? Was all this planned based on my book?

A cough beside her interrupted her musings, startling her so, that she about jumped out of her skin. Scanning the chapters of the book, she had been so engrossed in what she was reading, that she had failed to see the frail old lady sitting in the chair Mark had vacated minutes before.

Breathless, she said, "Jesus, Mary and Joseph! Where the heck did you come from? You scared the crap out of me!"

"I'm sorry dear. I saw you with your nose in that book." Hester looked at it pointedly. "I didn't want to scare you. I see that didn't work out so well now did it."

Abbi pushed her hair back from her face and noted the sadness on Hester's face. "It's okay. I'm just a bit jumpy. Lack of sleep will do that I guess..." She smiled. "Was there something you needed?"

"I've been so busy; I haven't had a chance to sit down with you and talk. To tell you, that I know why you're all here." The old woman smiled softly.

A foreboding feeling suddenly ran over Abbi's body. It had to be the house. It reminded Abbi of a vampire's lair, or was it something more?

"What do you mean Hester? I... I'm not following you."

"Do you mind if I tell you a story Abbi?"

Abbi shook her head. "Of course not. Please do."

"Well, it was an awfully long time ago. I was about your age; just a young woman."

Abbi's brows rose in surprise.

How old is she if she thinks I'm young?

"I was in love with a man. My goodness he was beautiful." A wistful smile crossed Hester's wrinkled face. "You see, he was sent to Germany to fight the war. I was so lost. Beside myself really." Melancholy flashed across her face as she looked down at her hands, her memories taking her back in time. "There was a scrimmage that his platoon was involved in. All of them perished that fateful day." A tear streaked down her soft cheek.

"Oh, my goodness!" Abbi reached out, laying her hand over Hester's. "I'm so sorry to hear that."

Hester looked at Abbi, and without batting an eyelash, said, "Oh don't be dear! I thought I would never see him again, but he came back to me. You see, he's still here." Hester glanced around the room, her eyes settling on the spot beside her. "He's sitting right next to me."

Whaaat?

Abbi had always believed in the idea of spirits walking the earth, especially ones taken so suddenly. But to hear that...

Oh, hell no!!

Abbi snatched her hand away as if she were burned by an invisible flame.

Hester leaned forward. "My Franklin told me you were coming here. And why..."

Okay, I've lost it... She did not just imply there was a ghost sitting beside her, did she?

Abbi giggled nervously. "Oh right! Well..." She nodded, feigning a yawn she let out a big stretch.... *The lady is off her rocker.*

"Um it was nice chatting with you Hester, but I think it's time I went to bed."

Not wanting it to appear that she was trying to make a hasty retreat, she slowly got up and walked towards the archway.

Hester turned watching her walk away. "Abbi... one more thing dear."

Abbi stopped, frozen to the spot. She dared not turn around for fear of seeing Franklin sitting beside the old woman.

"My Franklin told me to tell you. Ten miles to the east, then turn right. In the middle of... Slow down Franklin...!"

A tingling sensation skittered up Abbi's back, the hair on her neck rising as the seconds ticked by. She could feel the goosebumps dimple on her skin as if something were hovering behind her.

"Yes, yes I'll tell her! Abbi dear, he said, ten miles to the east, then turn right. It will take you to the middle of Sterling Forest. A lonely dirt trail passes through it called..." Hester paused as if waiting for something. Nodding she said, "Moonlit Road is what it's called. It winds along and ends at a long white building."

Ben told me it was a dirt road and a white building... It can't be...

Abbi slowly turned around. Hester was looking not at Abbi but into space. The space Abbi had just left.

"He also said it smells of skunk. Skunks? Why in heavens name would it smell like skunks?" Hester asked the empty air to her right.

Oh my God!!

Tears streamed down Abbi's cheeks. *It just can't be...*

Hester looked at her now, a worried look on her features. "Oh dear..."

In a panic, Abbi cried, "*What?!?* What did Franklin *say?*"

She knew she was going nuts, wanting answers from a 'ghost'. The room felt like it was spinning, and she in the middle of its vortex but she had to know what Franklin was saying.

"He said you will find who you're missing, there." Hester sighed. "You need to slow down Franklin." She looked to Abbi. "I'm sorry. He has so much to say he isn't making sense." Hester looked to the air at her right again. "Yes, yes. I'll tell her. He said one moonlit night is all it took?"

Oh Lord...How does she know?

Mark. Mark, had to have said something.

"He also said to tell you, all you want for Christmas is Ben?" Hester squinted and shrugged her frail shoulders. "Does that mean something to you?"

Abbi could feel the blood drain from her face as her knees buckled under her.

"Oh my! You need to hurry, Abbi. Ben doesn't have much time..."

Abbi had three choices. She could faint, she could scream and run through the house, or she could drive as fast as she could east and find that lonely dirt trail called Moonlit Road.

Immediately, she closed the distance between them. Abbi bent down and wrapped her arms around Hester's frail shoulders, hugging her to her, she said, "Thank you Hester, and please tell Franklin, I thank him eternally for all his help."

She quickly turned and ran up the stairs to wake the others.

Do I dare believe the ramblings of a lonely old woman? Your damned right I do!

To her knowledge, not one of them had mentioned Ben. And if they had, Ben and she were the only two who knew what she wanted for Christmas...

Chapter 12

The vehicle was flying down the road with Abbi at the wheel in the dead of the night. Once again, all five of them were loaded into the SUV, headed on a wild goose chase.

After running up the stairs of Hester's home, Abbi quickly shook everyone awake, telling them they had to go now. The only way to get them motivated was to tell them she wasn't coming back. In less than five minutes they were all piling into the vehicle.

"Now where in hell are we going, Abbi?" Kim yawned tiredly from the passenger seat. "And will you put your damn window up?!"

"Sorry, if I close it, I'll miss the turnoff."

Mark, Ava, and Tim where all huddled together for warmth in the back seat. Mark leaned close to Ava, his mouth mere inches from her ear.

"If we don't find Ben soon, you do realize we are going to have to take drastic measures, right?"

Ava nodded in silent agreement. She was in denial that her mother was losing it. But her mom's actions were now speaking louder than any words ever could. Her mother would disown her, Ava knew that, but Abbi was leaving them little choice...

"There!!" Abbi pointed as she slowed the vehicle down. "Kim, what does that road sign say?"

"It's too dark to see." Kim reached for the door handle and shoved the door open. "Hang on a second."

The logical thing to do would have been to drive along side of the sign, but no one was logical at that moment in time. Ambling over to the post, Kim stopped, and looked up at the sign. She swung her head back towards the vehicle, shouted something and motioned to the sky, then pointed to the road.

"What in the hell is she doing?" Tim asked.

Ava leaned forward to get a better look at her aunt. "Ah...I don't know."

Mark opened his window and yelled, "This isn't the time for charades, Kim!"

Abbi glanced at the clock on the display. 4:03 am. They had to hurry. She stepped on the gas and steered towards Kim. "What did it say?" she asked, pulling aside Kim.

"I was trying to tell you it's called Moonlit Road...I thought one of you would have figured out the reference of me pointing to the moon and the road." She huffed as she climbed in and slammed the door closed.

Abbi didn't move a muscle. Franklin had said Moonlit Road, the only problem with that was he didn't say which way...left or right.

She threw the gearshift into park. Turning in her seat she looked at all of them one by one.

"Guys I have something to tell you... you're likely going to think I'm crazy. And I don't blame you if you do." She paused wondering how she would put it in a way that sounded less absurd.

"I...Hester and I had a talk tonight. She told me a story. How she had been in love with a man that was called to war."

She took a deep breath. "Um, he died. Over in Germany I think she said. Anyway, he came back to her..." Abbi put a hand to her head.

My God this even sounds crazy to me!

She giggled. "He still lives there... err... well he's there with her. Anyhow, he told her to tell me where to find Ben." She looked at each one, then rushed on. "And so here we are."

They all had 'the look'. The look of how they could have her committed without her knowledge.

"I know what you're thinking. I'm crazy, right? I swear on Ben's life, I'm not. Franklin told her things that she couldn't possibly have known."

Kim broke the silence first. "Franklin? Who is Franklin?"

"Franklin is Hester's love." Mark answered. "*Wait*! No this is *wrong*! Abbi sweets, I know more than anyone else what you're going through right now. But you have to stop this!"

Abbi's throat stung. Try as she might to fight it, her eyes filled, the tears slipped down her cheeks in rivers. She had been fighting so desperately to not cry, but having Mark doubt her of all people, was more than she could take.

Her lips quivered. "Mark, you have no idea what I've gone through, what I'm going through every day since Ben has been gone." She felt like screaming her lungs out but didn't have the energy to do so. She pointed a finger at him, jabbing the air. "Don't you *dare* sit there and tell me that you do." Her voice broke on a sob as her gaze raked over each one of them. "*None* of you know what I am going through, and I pray to God you never do."

She turned back and laid her forehead on the steering wheel. Silent sobs wracked her body. She shouldn't have said that to Mark. He was only trying to help.

Ava reached out a hand, rubbing Abbi's back, she said, "Mom? What did Franklin tell Hester?"

Without moving, Abbi took a steadying breath. Sniffling, she said, "He told her to tell me to go ten miles to the east, then turn right. It will take you to the middle of Sterling Forest, he said."

Everyone in the vehicle but Abbi looked out the windows...

They were in the middle of a forest.

Wide eyed, Kim said, "There was a sign when we turned on this road that said Sterling Forest."

"Yes. And a lonely dirt trail passes through it called..." Abbi squeezed her eyes shut. "Moonlit road. It will wind along to a white building. That smells of skunks..."

"Skunks!" Ava muttered.

"Pot plants I bet," Tim said.

"Yeah. Ben told me it was filled with marijuana. They call it *The Farm*." Abbi leaned back in her seat. She looked up, trance-like, she continued. "Franklin told Hester that I'll find who I'm missing there."

She turned in her seat to look at Mark. "He told Hester what Ben wrote on that note."

"What...wait." A puzzled look settled on his face, then his brows shot skyward as he gripped the back of her seat. "*How?!*"

Abbi sighed and shrugged her shoulders, "I thought maybe you mentioned it."

"I swear Abbi, I didn't breathe a word of it to anyone."

She was back in her trance. "He also knew what I wanted for Christmas..."

"Which is...?" Kim asked.

Before Abbi could answer, all their cellphones went off at once.

Everyone, except Tim searched their pockets. As one, they all said the same thing. "Ben...?"

"Bingo..." Was all Abbi had to say. Going with her gut instinct, she put the vehicle in drive, cranked the steering wheel left and gunned the engine. "Someone quick. Read me that text please?"

"I'm so sorry Abbi, for ever doubting you." Mark blubbered from the back.

"It's okay. I would've doubted me too if I were you."

Abbi took her eyes off the road for a second to look at her sister. "Kim?"

"Yeah Abbi?"

Nodding towards the phone in Kim's hand, she asked, "Can you read me that text?"

"Oh! Right. Sure thing." Kim looked down at her phone and cleared her throat. "'*Hi back at you love.*'" Kim felt tears come to her eyes. Waving a hand in front of her face, she said, "Ava, you read it."

Abbi looked in the rear-view mirror. Ava's face too was wet with tears.

What in the world did Ben say? I should have read it myself...

Seeing how Ava would be no help, Abbi determined Mark wouldn't be either. Every so often she could hear a sniff coming from his direction.

"Ava, honey, give Tim your phone to read. Tim, would you?" Abbi asked.

"Sure, I'll do that," he said, taking the phone from Ava. "Okay, here goes. '*Hi back at you love. I'm letting you know that I will be leaving here tonight. I need to. I just had to let you know that you may get a call from the 'boss man'. They are going to demand a ransom from you...*' Abbi, I think you need to pull over," Tim said, quietly.

There was no way she was pulling over, the road was just starting to wind, any minute the white building would come into view.

She shook her head. "No. Keep reading Tim."

He sighed. "Alright than... '*Don't pay it Abbi. They have every intention of killing me at dawn*.'"

Abbi's foot slipped off the gas pedal.

Heaven, help me, maybe I should pull over? No, I have to keep going.

"Sorry," she mumbled. Stepping on the gas even more.

Tim continued. "'*I should mention who the 'boss man' is. He's a cop. A Sheriff. Jack Martin. Do NOT trust him Abbi*'... Holy Shit!" Tim shouted. "I did trust that dude."

"Let me see that." Mark grabbed the cell out of Tim's hand and picked up where Tim had ended. "'*I have some help from Smitty/Calvin. I know what you're thinking, but my gut says I can trust him. I must trust him, with my leg, I have little choice... I need to go now sweet one. Remember always, that I've loved you since that moonlit night, Ben.*'"

Silence followed. Abbi swiped the blinding tears away. It wouldn't do Ben any good if she were to crash when they were so close to him.

"911? I'm calling to report that a police officer has been shot out on Moonlit Road." Everyone looked at Tim but Abbi. A huge grin was pasted on his face.

"Mhm... yes just turn left at the crossroads, follow it to the white building. You can't miss it from the smell of skunks. My name?" Tim started fumbling with the speaker. "Sorry, you're breaking up..." He then hit the end button.

Grinning, he looked up and saw all eyes on him.

"What?? It's the fastest way to get the cops to come."

"Good to know." Kim chuckled, as she wiped her eyes.

Abbi pulled the SUV onto the shoulder, angling it between the trees. She looked around before cutting the engine. It was the perfect spot. No one would be able to see it if they happened to look down the road. "Let's hope they get here quick."

Five hundred feet give or take a few, sat a low white building close to the road. The smell of skunks permeated the air.

"What should we do?" Ava whispered.

"I know what I'm not going to do," Abbi said. Soundlessly, she opened her door. "I'm not waiting for the cops to show up." She quietly closed it and walked to the back of the SUV.

"Abbi get the hell back in the car." Tim hissed.

She ignored him. Opening the rear door, she looked in the compartment.

Where would I find the tire iron?

Lifting the hatch of the cargo area, she found what she was looking for. Snatching it up, she tested the weight of it. Giving a self-satisfied nod, she looked up to see four sets of eyes staring back at her. "What?"

They all spoke at once.

"Mom. What are you doing?"

"Abbi sweets, you can't possibly be thinking of doing what I think you're thinking of doing?"

"Abbi, I said get the hell back in the car and wait for the cops!"

Kim the only logical one of the four, said, "Don't you dare leave without me!!" Scrambling out of the car, she joined Abbi at the back of the vehicle. Poking around in the cargo area, she triumphantly whisper shouted, "Aha!" And held up the jack.

Mark snorted. "What are you going to do with that? Change their tire?"

Kim stood for a minute in thought. "Well... I'll whack them over the head," she said.

Mark rolled his eyes and looked at Tim. Both men nodded as they reached for their door handles and joined Abbi and Kim at the back of the SUV.

"If you're all going, I am too. But you can't just storm in there expecting to find Ben." Ava reasoned. "And why the need of weapons? How bad can it be in there?"

Abbi shook her head. "Ava, I'm not waiting another second, and they have guns. That's why I need you to stay here. Wait for the cops, okay?"

Ava grunted her protest. "No, I'm coming. I'll be fine." She moved to slide out the door.

"Ava... I don't need you there." Abbi paused at how horrible that sounded. "I meant... I don't need to worry about you too, okay? Please, just stay in the car, lock the doors and wait for the police." Not waiting for a response, Abbi closed the hatch with a soft thud.

"Tim, can you lead the way to that building?" Abbi jerked her head in the direction of it. "We need to get behind it, I think. Ben said there are cabins back there."

In a loud whisper he said, "Follow me, stay close. And if you hear gunshots for the love of God, duck."

Chapter 13

"Tim how much further is it?" Kim scrunched her nose and wheezed as she leaned against a tree.

"Shhhh!" He held his hand out as he hunched over, peering through the trees.

"Do you see anything?" Abbi asked softly. Squatting down, she too looked through the trees.

They were in the forest at the back of the building. The moon gave off enough light to see a row of cabins standing silent against the backdrop of more trees. Right in the middle of a clearing.

Abbi's breath caught in her throat at the sight before her eyes. There, a man, and a woman were talking. Both had their arms raised, both with a gun in their hand. The man was pointing his gun at the woman's head. But the woman was pointing hers in the opposite direction.

So, who is she pointing it at?

Staring intently, Abbi silently moved closer to get a better angle. It was an old woman, it had to be Daisy! Dread filled her as she took one step closer. It felt like a cold icy hand, gripped Abbi's heart as her eyes fell on the man wearing a bright yellow coat. *Ben!*

Her heart dropped to the pit of her stomach. She had known with every fiber in her body who Daisy was pointing that gun at...but she didn't want to believe that it could only be Ben. Seeing him standing there with a gun aimed at him...

She had to act. She couldn't stand there a second longer and watch the man she loved was shot through the heart. She scurried off towards the trio.

"Abbi get the hell back here!" Tim hissed.

"I'll get her." Mark called out in hot pursuit.

Abbi was within reach, just one more stride and Mark would have her. She stopped dead in her tracks, causing him all but to topple over her. Somehow, he managed to stop himself before hitting the ground.

"What the hell Ab...!" Mark was quickly cut off by Abbi's hand over his mouth. She pointed to the edge of the trees to her left as a second man exited into the clearing.

They watched in silence as he approached the gun happy group from behind. Mark turned to Abbi, a horrified look in his eyes. Eyes that popped out of his head when he saw the guy draw not one, but two guns from his waistband.

BEN SAW A FIGURE APPROACH from behind Dean and Daisy. *God please don't let it be Abbi...*

He was relieved when he saw Smitty come into view.

Smitty held a finger to his lips. Quietly he reached behind him with both hands. Quickly he brought them forward, a gun in each, one aimed at Dean, the other at Daisy. A twig snapped under his boot causing both to turn to face him.

"Why don't you gimme that gun there, before it goes off, hmm Daisy?" Smitty said, nodding at the gun in her hand. "Ben, get behind me," he called out.

Without a word, Ben started to make his way over. With every step he took, he braced for the sound of gunshots ringing out; followed by a piercing pain. It felt an eternity, but he was almost there.

Daisy glared at Smitty. "What the hell is wrong with you?" Not moving an inch, she held fast to the gun, still aiming it at Ben. Her voice shook with anger. "This isn't part of our plan."

"No, you're right, it isn't part of *your* plan. Now drop the gun!" he yelled.

"Why? What difference does it make if he dies now or at dawn?" she demanded as her hand shook uncontrollably.

Dean spoke up. "All in good time old woman. The Sheriff said dawn, he has his reasons for it I suspect."

"Shut up!!" She screamed. Motioning at Ben with the gun. "You know I have a job to do and it's to take him out by any means," she said as she took aim...

ABBI AND MARK WERE joined by the others at the edge of the clearing. All watched in stunned silence as both Daisy and the other man jerked around to the newest member of their gathering.

A soft sob escaped past Abbi's lips when she heard Ben's name. Holding her breath, listening to the gravel crunch under the slow rhythmic shuffling of his crutches was more that she could handle. Tears glistened down her cheeks as she watched him slowly come into view. The sight of him tore her to pieces, he looked broken in so many ways.

Abbi's eyes snapped to Daisy when she heard the woman screaming. As if in slow motion, she watched the old woman take aim at Ben.

"Nooooo!!" Abbi shrieked as she crashed through the trees, the others hot on her heels.

There was no way the gun happy group didn't hear them. The fierce cry of anguish that came from Abbi's soul would have had the hounds of hell running in fear. They looked like crazed lunatics, brandishing their weapons as they came into the clearing to the sound of sirens approaching in the distance.

The welcoming sound of the police didn't stop Abbi, she went straight for Daisy; the only one holding a gun to Ben's head. Her only thought was to cause as much pain Ben had endured at their hands, to her. The fact that Daisy swung the gun in her direction didn't stop her either. Abbi wanted to maim her, pull her hair out from the roots, and then punch her in the face. She might even throw the tire iron at her.

Ben stood rooted to the spot.

Abbi don't you see the gun in her hand?

Seeing that look on her face, he knew he had to stop her.

"Abbi, no!" he yelled, launching himself in her direction just as a shot rang out. He didn't make it in time. He watched as Abbi collapsed on the ground, her blood pooling underneath her.

Memories of them together flashed through his mind like an old family video on a projection screen. An animalistic howl of pain came from Ben as he fell to his knees by her side.

His tears mingled with Abbi's blood on her face. He checked her pulse... nothing. He gathered her into his arms and rocked her back and forth while his screams of agony echoed in the clearing.

The anguish he felt a moment before only intensified the malice he was now feeling. He set his venomous stare on Daisy. Tenderly, he laid Abbi on the ground, and slowly raised to his full height... without the aid of his crutches. He heard a loud gasp behind him. Thinking it was Kim reacting over finding Abbi, he forged on.

Mark knew what Ben was going to do. He had broken up a fair share of fights in his lifetime. Ben's included. Despite what the circumstances were, he knew Ben could never live with himself if he took out his anger on a woman. Especially a little old lady.

Mark grabbed him from behind, wrapping an arm around his chest he pulled him back. "It's not worth it buddy, you can't do this. She's an old lady," Mark said hotly against the back of Ben's neck.

Ben fought to loosen Marks's grip. Truth be told he didn't have the strength to do so.

"She isn't an old woman! She's wearing a mask." Ben spat, still twisting, and turning trying desperately to get out of Mark's grasp.

Kim came around them, with tears in her eyes she said, "No Ben. You can't...but I can." She put her hand on his chest and shoved him back. She promptly turned and sneered at Daisy, "You're lucky she's alive. You better hope she stays that way, bitch!" She flung the jack she was still holding at Daisy like it was a shot put.

Daisy cried out in surprise. Not expecting a solid steel object to be hurled at her, she dropped the gun and tried to catch the jack before it crashed into her. She failed miserably, howling in pain as it landed on her foot with a sickening, bone cracking thud.

Ben grabbed Kim by the arms just as the first of many police cruiser pulled into the clearing.

"Kim, did you say Abbi's alive?"

Kim nodded. "She must have had the wind knocked out of her when she hit the ground. Didn't you hear her gasping?"

Mark gave a tug on Ben's arm. "Hey, how come you remember her, but you don't me?" he asked.

Ben shook his head in answer to Kim and ignored Mark as he stumbled to Abbi's side. He laid his head against her chest. Holding his breath, he prayed Kim was right.

A single tear slipped across the bridge of his nose, blinding him momentarily. He closed his eyes as he felt Abbi's heartbeat, steady against his cheek. A shuttering sob escaped past his lips when he felt her hand make its way to his hair, to stoke it softly.

"Abbi. Abbi, can you hear me?" He looked at her face. His hand made its way to gently cradle her head as if she were a newborn baby.

"Ben?" she mumbled, opening her eyes. She tried to sit up. Wincing as the pain shot through her head. She put a hand to her temple, feeling a sticky warmth. Confused, she pulled her hand away and looked at it. Blood. "What happened?"

"You were shot. A bullet grazed your head," he said, gently gathering her in his arms. He inhaled her scent deeply as he held her. "You weren't breathing... just bleeding. The medics are here now," he whispered, as he put an arm under her knees and drew her to his chest.

"I've got you sweet one." He stood up, holding her as the paramedics came with a stretcher. Gently he laid her on it and backed away. Watching as they worked on her.

Mark came to him. Putting an arm around Ben's shoulder he gave it a squeeze.

"She'll be all right, buddy. What about you though? Shouldn't you be getting looked at yourself?"

Someone shouting prevented Ben from answering him.

"Let me through! I need to see my mother now!" Ava yelled, shoving at the police officer blocking her way.

"It's okay Billy, let her through." Smitty hollered to the police officer.

"Ava, over here." Mark waved her over towards him and Ben.

"Ben!" She flung herself at him, hugging him with all her might. "I'm so happy to see you're safe."

"It's good to see you, Ava." Taking a step back, he set her at arm's length, his eyes full of worry were focused on something over her shoulder. "Ah I need to know. How was your mom, while I was gone?"

Ava turned her head and glanced to see what Ben was looking at. The medics were wrapping a large white bandage around Abbi's head.

Not that he doubted for a minute that she missed him. His only concern was it hadn't affected Abbi too drastically. It didn't matter to him one way or the other. Nothing could kill the love he had for her. He needed to know if her feelings were the same for him.

"Honestly?" Ava raised a brow at him. He looked at her and nodded.

"Well. I've never seen her so upset in my life. She was going nuts. I saved mental health crisis numbers in my phone just in case. You have no idea how many times I almost called them."

"What stopped you?" Ben asked.

"We never left her alone." She sighed and pointed towards Abbi. "I'm just going to go over to her now." She excused herself and left.

"Ben, can I ask a question?" Mark looked directly at him.

Ben looked at him and nodded. "Of course."

Ava returned before Mark could get a word out, she put a hand on Ben's arm and said, "She's asking for you."

Torn between going to Abbi's side and Mark he said, "Please tell her I'm coming. I'll just be a moment." Ben turned back to Mark. "You were saying...?"

Mark frowned. "How come you know Ava and Kim, but you don't have a clue who I am..."

Ben stood in thought. Finally, he said, "You know, Abbi and I never did go on that date you paid for." The relief on his friend's face was all Ben needed to see. He gave Mark a smirk as he limped towards the ambulance.

Stopping he turned and looked at Mark.

I wonder...

"Ah... Mark? Does the name Everett mean anything to you?"

Mark looked taken aback. "Doesn't it to you? Ben, buddy. That's your stage name..."

Ben frowned. "Oh, right. Um, aren't you coming?" He asked, jerking a thumb towards Abbi.

Mark sauntered over and put an arm around his friend. "Wouldn't miss it for the world."

"Say... do you still have that box I gave you on the plane?"

"Box?" Mark raised a brow. "What bo... Oh shit! I gave it to Abbi. She has it!"

"Oh okay. Well, I'll just go buy her a new one then."

As they passed a police cruiser, Daisy was screaming from the back about her rights for medical attention.

"Ma'am, right now you will need to wait your turn. You gave up your rights when you killed an FBI agent and attempted to kill two innocent people." The police officer slammed the door shut and walked to Dean and Smitty, muttering to them about the loud one in her car. Ben's step faltered.

Wait a minute... Why is Dean not in a cruiser...? His question was answered when he saw the flash of a metal star on Dean's belt.

His thoughts were interrupted from a quick jab of Mark's elbow to his ribs. They had arrived at the back of the ambulance.

"Hey," Ben said softly, his eyes matching his tone. He looked at her laying on the stretcher, the blue blanket tucked to her chin. She was beautiful to him even with her bandaged head and pale skin.

"Hi." A smile tugged at the corners of her lips.

"Sir?" A small female voice spoke behind him. He turned and looked down. "My name is Allison I'm a medic. You're injured, too, aren't you?"

Ben nodded. His leg was hurting, but nothing close to what it had been. It must have only been sprained. The bulge under the skin had been nothing more than swelling. With absolutely nothing to do the past week and a half gave it time to heal, he supposed.

"We will take you along with Abbi here if you're okay with that. Hop in." Allison waited until Ben climbed in and sat down. Slamming the door shut, she went around to get in next to her partner.

"Do you know who that is Reece?" Allison asked, as she shut her door and buckled up.

"Yeah. That's Ben Everett. Awesome actor."

Allison wrinkled her nose. "Who? What...no, I meant the lady," she replied, smiling. She too was in awe of who they were transporting to the hospital in Gatlinburg.

"Oh...no, I have no idea," he said as he steered down the winding dirt road.

"It's Abbi Stevens... The author of the Jasper Killings?" She smiled as she turned to check on their patients. Her heart melted at the sight of them. There, Ben sat on the floor, his head on Abbi's chest, staring at her while he spoke softly. Their hands clasped as he stroked her hair with his other.

Allison turned back in her seat. "Someday, I hope to find a love like that." She sighed wistfully as the ambulance made its way down the road.

Part Two

Chapter 14

B en couldn't take his eyes off her. She mesmerized him. If he had any doubts before of where he wanted his life to take him, it was all clear as crystal now. Wherever Abbi was, he was home.

Trying desperately to stay awake, Abbi rubbed his back.

"Ben?"

"Yes, love?"

"Hold me?"

"Of course, sweet one," he whispered as he rose off the floor. Feeling weak as a kitten, she moved towards the wall of the ambulance with his help. Ben laid down beside her and gently wrapped her in his arms. She laid her head against his chest wincing at the pain it caused, but nothing was stopping her from being held in his arms.

"After we leave the hospital, can we please go home?" She asked, her eyes fluttering shut.

She was so incredibly tired. Bone tired. She felt Ben shift. Opening one eye she looked up at him, mere inches from her face.

"Yes, Abbi. The bullet just grazed you from what the medics told me. So as soon as you're released to travel, we'll go home." He kissed the tip of her nose. "Sleep now, I'm not going anywhere, anymore," he murmured, pressing his lips to her hair.

She didn't want to sleep. She was afraid that if she did, it would all be a dream, like so many before.

She looked up at him again. The tears she had held on to for so long now threatened to spill over at any second.

"I've missed you so much. I thought that you were gone forever."

"I've missed you too. Now, hush love. I'm here." He kissed her cheek. "I promise, I'll never go anywhere without you again." His lips trailed to her ear, along her jawline to her mouth.

Abbi welcomed his touch. She instantly melted against him as he deepened the kiss. A bump in the road, reminded them exactly where they were.

He leaned back and stared at her.

"I can't stop looking at you. You're the most beautiful person I've ever had the privilege of knowing. On the inside and more stunning on the out.

He laid a finger against her lips when she was working on arguing the fact. "Shh, I never say anything I don't mean. And I meant every word of it." He gazed into her eyes. It was time.

"Abbi...I wanted to do this the proper way. Me on one knee, with a box in my hand." He paused. "But I'm not waiting another second for things to be perfect."

Abbi reached under the blanket, blindly searching for her jacket pocket. Fumbling with the blanket, she finally got her arm free. She opened her hand, revealing the small box within.

"Is this it? Mark gave me this when he was still in the hospital. He made me promise not to open it and to give it back to you when we found you." She looked up at him through her lashes. "I swear I didn't open it."

He grinned. "I believe you." Ben took it from her hand. With her still wrapped in his arms, he opened it.

There siting in the middle of the velvety box was a band of silver. A stunning diamond sat nestled in the middle, encircled by peridots and topaz.

"Oh...!" Abbi looked at him.

Ben took a deep steadying breath and tried to settle the racing of his heart.

Why am I so nervous?

Deep down he knew why. They had never talked about marriage before, and he was afraid of her answer.

He swallowed hard. "Abbi, will you give me the greatest honour of my life in becoming my wife?" He held his breath, waiting for her answer.

With him looking so lovingly into her eyes, Abbi wondered how she could have ever doubted his feelings for her.

Wait... Did I hear him right? He did not just ask me to marry him...did he?

Abbi was speechless.

She shook her head slowly from side to side, her eyes never leaving his. When she saw the disappointment flash across his handsome face, her face crumpled. "Dear lord, I didn't mean no! You shocked me; I didn't know it was an engagement ring. Mark never told me."

She took hold of his coat, giving it a slight tug, she urged him closer. Smiling, she whispered, "Yes. I will." Then tenderly laid her lips on his.

Her kiss stole his breath away as he inhaled her intoxicating scent as the ambulance pulled to a stop.

"We're here guys." Reece called out as he put the gearshift in park.

"I better get a move on it hadn't I?" Ben moved off the stretcher and kneeled beside it, taking the ring from the box. "Shall I?" he asked, taking her hand in his.

She nodded. A soft smile on her lip as he gently placed the ring on her finger.

"I had it specially made," he said softly, looking into her eyes. "The diamond is for April, the month we met, and when I fell in love with you. The topaz is for November, your birthstone. And the peridots are for..."

"Your eyes." Abbi breathed. "They remind me of your eyes."

He chuckled. "No, it's my birthstone."

"I know, but they still remind me of your eyes."

She smiled as the back door opened.

"Let's get you folks looked at, shall we?" Reese said, reaching to unlock the wheels on the stretcher. He said to Ben as he pulled Abbi from the back of the ambulance, "Mr. Everett, you sit tight. Allison will be right back with a wheelchair for you."

Everett...Everett

Ben thought a wheelchair was a little extreme but nodded. "Sure thing." It gave him time to be alone with his thoughts.

Something had been bugging him since the farm. What was it that Daisy had said? She'd had a job to do...

Clearly it was to kill me but who ordered it and who was she talking to on the phone that night?

He dared not mention it to Abbi. Then again, she may have heard it the way she had come charging at Daisy like she had. That was another thing... Who the hell was Daisy?

He felt a hand gently shaking his arm. Glancing down he saw Allison there, an empty wheelchair waiting beside her.

Concern was etched across her face. "Mr. Everett? Are you okay?"

"Ah. Yeah. Sorry." He sighed, heaving himself off the seat.

Allison hurriedly grabbed his arm. "Here, let me help you."

Together, they managed to get him settled in the chair. Allison unlocked the wheels, just as a blinding light flashed in their eyes.

"Dammit! Who the hell told them?" She muttered, turning Ben around so that her back was all they could see.

"Is that a photographer?" Ben queried, looking around Allison to see.

"No, it's the paparazzi. They have been hanging around the hospital since the crash, waiting like vultures."

Quickly she wheeled him into the emergency department, down a hall and stopped at the nurses' station. Nodding towards the doors that her and Ben had just come through, she said, "You might want to lock those doors and get security out there. The scavengers are back..." All at once four nurses jumped up, running for the doors.

Allison nodded, pushed the wheelchair forward and said, "Now. Let's get you to Abbi."

SHE WAS SLEEPING WHEN Ben was brought into her cubicle. A doctor was standing over her looking at her chart while a nurse checked her vitals.

"Hi Doc. This is Dr. Anderson," Allison whispered loudly to Ben. "This here is Ben, he's with Abbi." She pushed his wheelchair next to the bed. "He needs his leg looked at. Looks to be either a bad strain or a hairline fracture. He was walking on it." She looked around at Ben "Right? You were walking on it?"

He nodded. "Yes. A bit."

"Nurse, can you order an x-ray for Mr..... ah..." Dr. Anderson flipped through the papers Allison had handed him. He looked at Ben, questioningly.

"Quinn. Ben Quinn," he supplied.

"Mr. Quinn, please?" He finished addressing the nurse.

Dr. Anderson came around the foot of Abbi's bed to Ben and knelt in front of him.

"Any pain or swelling?" Not waiting for a response, he pulled up Ben's pant leg and felt along his calf muscle. Frowning, he looked up at him. "How long has it been like this?"

"Ah. It happened in the crash. About a week and a half now?" Ben answered.

"I don't think it's too serious, you were able to walk on it. The x-ray will tell us more." He stood up and wrote on a chart. "We ordered some blood tests on Abbi; they should be ready by the time you come back from the imaging department."

"Will she be okay?" Ben asked anxiously, looking at her still form.

"The bullet grazed slightly above her temple. She's lucky, any lower and she wouldn't be here." The doctor said solemnly.

"There was so much blood..." Ben said, staring blankly at the memory.

Dr. Anderson nodded in agreement. "Head wounds will do that. My concern is when she fell. Did she hit her head or land on her stomach?"

Oh god, is he worried about internal bleeding?

"Um." Ben thought for a second. "Neither. She just crumpled. Like she passed out. She did land on her back, but I don't think she hit her head."

"She wasn't breathing, is that right?"

"Kim. Her sister said the wind was knocked out of her. I thought she was gone..." He blinked the sting away as he relived the scene in his mind.

Ben watched, as the doctor wrote on Abbi's chart. He was doing an awful lot of writing.

When he could no longer stand it, he asked, "Is there a problem Doctor?"

Dr Anderson, put her chart on the peg at the end of her bed. He turned and looked at Ben. "No, not at all. Just want to make sure her levels are where they should be and that they keep rising. She will be moved to a private room. I'll keep her for a couple of days to monitor her blood periodically through-out it."

Ben frowned. "Levels? What sort of levels?"

The doctor smiled. "Why, her hCG levels of course."

"And they are...?" Ben hedged for an answer.

"To make sure she doesn't miscarry." The doctor said.

At this point Ben was totally confused, shaking his head he squinted. "Miscarry? What does she miss carrying?"

Doctor Anderson let out a bark of laughter. "You know... a baby?" His brows rose on the last word.

"Oh." Ben nodded his head. "Okay...Wait..." He half stood up. "A *what?!*"

Glancing at Abbi, laying so peacefully there, a smile widened on his mouth. He couldn't believe what the doctor said. "Y.. you mean she's pregnant? You're saying that I'm going to be a father? You said that, right?"

"Well. I guess you are if you and she are together. Yes, that's what I'm saying." The doctor nodded. Walking over to the door he stopped. "Now that we have that covered. Congratulations! Nurse Murray, will give you a tetanus shot and take you to x-ray."

Ben looked at the nurse who was standing there with a syringe in hand and beamed. "I'm going to be a father."

"So, I heard. Congrats. Now stand up there and drop your pants."

Ben did as he was told. The stupid grin never faltered from his face; not even when the needle jabbed into his butt cheek.

Chapter 15

Dean had just left. He had stopped by wanting to see how Abbi was doing and left his card and told Ben to reach out if either of them needed anything.

Ben was still reeling from the shock of finding out the man was a US Marshal. He was still trying to wrap it around his head that Dean's tough guy act had been just that, an act. Ben told him he should get into acting; he was that convincing.

Now he was sitting beside Abbi's hospital bed, watching the steady rise and fall of her chest. The day nurse Paige had brought him in a reclining chair after he refused to leave her side. Paige said it was of the utmost importance to keep his leg raised. The x-ray revealed a fracture of the fibula. The wrap job Daisy did at least saved it from further damage. Luckily, he was on the mend, and the walking boot cast would allow him to walk without the need of crutches most of the time.

As he watched her sleep, he couldn't help but think of his timing to ask her to marry him; before either of them found out about the baby. Otherwise, she might have thought that was the only reason he'd asked.

Maybe she already knew?

No. She would have told him he was sure of it. Her groaning in her sleep had him on high alert.

Ben quietly put the footrest down on the chair. Moving to the edge of the seat, he waited to see if she would stir some more, that way he could be there for her if she did. He watched as a frown appeared on her face, while her legs kicked at some unforeseeable force.

He gently leaned on the edge of the bed and reached for her hand. Leisurely he traced circles on her palm, as his other hand reached to smooth her hair back from her face. A single tear ran from her closed eyes. His thumb followed the path it made, making him want nothing more than to crawl into bed beside her and hold her. He'd already tried that and was told he couldn't. The real reason for the chair being brought in for him, he suspected.

ABBI SO DESPERATELY wanted to reach out to Ben. That bitch was between the two of them. Holding a gun to his head; preventing her from reaching him. She had to do something, anything to stop her from shooting him. She watched in horror as the bullet sliced through the air in slow motion, only stopping as it plunged into Ben's chest...

She screamed his name and bolted upright in the bed.

Ben jumped back causing the bed to shake. "*Bloody hell, Abbi!*" He nearly shouted, remembering the last second that they were in a hospital. Softening his tone, he murmured, "Love, are you okay?" One minute he was drying her tears, the next she was screaming at him.

She was scaring the hell out of him. She was looking through him, not at him. "Abbi? Honey are you okay. Do you want me to get the doctor?" He stood for a moment, nodding, he said, "I'll get the doctor."

"No! I'm fine, it was just a dream... a nightmare," she said finally coming to her senses.

He wasn't convinced she could see him. The way she had looked at him, as if he weren't even there.

"Really Ben, I'm fine. Can you get me a drink of water please?"

"Sure, love." He went to the table on the other side of her bed to fetch her a glass of water.

"You're walking! What did they say about your leg?" She asked as he held the glass to her lips.

He chuckled. "I am yes. It's on the mend. Got myself this fancy boot." He lifted his leg for her to see as she took a sip of water.

She felt terrible. Here she was lying in a bed while he limped around with a cast on his leg, waiting on her. But goodness she was exhausted. She tossed the covers aside. Intent on getting dressed and going home.

"Um Abbi, where are you going?"

"Why home. I'm going home Ben. Where are my clothes?" she asked, slowly coming to a stand.

"In the closet, but.... ah, you can't," he said and went to stand in front of her.

"Of course, I can. I'm fine. A bit woozy but I'll come around." She ducked around him, headed to the closet.

"No, you need to get back in bed. You know, you lost a lot of blood." He took hold of her shoulders and steered her around back towards the bed.

"Ben don't be so silly. It's time we went home."

He didn't want to come right out and say Abbi your pregnant, but what little choice was she giving him? The doctor had to watch her levels.

A moment of panic seized him.

What if she doesn't want a baby?

He never thought about that. She already had kids, grown ones; would she want to take care of a newborn after so much time had passed? He suddenly felt sick to his stomach.

As much as he loved the idea of being a father, he couldn't make her have his child... or could he? No. He wasn't the one that would be pregnant for nine months. Despite that he loved the idea of being a father; he loved her more. If there was any risk to her, he would refuse to allow her to take it. He was being selfish in that respect. But so be it. It was settled at least from his point of view. He would only support her decision if there was absolutely no risk to her.

"Love, you need to sit down. We have to talk."

Abbi looked at him, really looked at him. He was scaring the hell out of her. Was there something so terribly wrong with her that she didn't know about?

"Ben... what's wrong? Am I sick?"

Is he sick?! Oh no... No!

She couldn't handle it if he were. Had everything taken a toll on him more than she'd realized? Now she felt such an incredible guilt. She sat down on the edge of the bed. Staring down at the ring he had given her. The ring he so thoughtfully had made just for them. She breathed in a shaky breath and searched his face. "Are you?"

"God no!" He sat down on the bed beside her and pulled her close. "No Abbi, neither one of us is." He smoothed his cheek on her silky hair careful to avoid the bandage. He took her chin in his hand and turned her face upwards, to look into her eyes.

"Then tell me why I need to stay." She felt like she was on the verge of tears, like a tired child being told no. "Why can't we go home right—"

His mouth covering hers swallowed the rest of her words. Someone coughed loudly. Ben broke off the kiss and leaned his forehead against hers. "One second," he murmured, brushing his lips where his head rested seconds before. Abbi watched as he went to the door, talking in a hushed tone to the nurse standing there, a plastic caddy in her hands.

Ben closed the door soundlessly and returned to sit back down beside Abbi.

"What the hell is going on Ben?"

"Um." He scratched his head, wondering just how he was going to tell her. He pointed to the door. "She'll be back."

Abbi raised her brows. "Okay... *And?!*" She watched the play of emotions cross his face as he stared at the opposite wall. What really confused her was the stupid grin on his face. She watched as he physically wiped the smile off his face with his hand, then finally, he turned to her.

"And... ah." He stopped. Feeling confident, he steepled his fingers... quickly he leaned forward rubbing the bridge of his nose.

Nope I can't bring myself to say it. What if she's mad? What if she blames me, then what? He shook his head. No, she wouldn't do that.

"Ben for the love of God, will you just *spit it out*?" She raised her voice he noted on the last three words.

His eyes snapped to hers. She was getting a bit upset he could see. He took a deep breath, took her hands in his and rubbed his thumbs back and forth, hoping her anger would diminish.

He looked deeply into her eyes and said, "Abbi... we never talked about this. Ever. But." She looked so beautiful staring at him.

Why am I worrying when she looks at me this way?

A smile tugged at the corner of his lips. "We are going to have a baby, you and I."

Oh no...

He watched as her face went from serene to scrunched up confusion, then shock. Her body began shaking uncontrollably. He watched as she leaned forward clutching her stomach. *The BABY!!*

Afraid she would topple onto the floor he grabbed her from behind. That's when he realized she wasn't in shock. On no not Abbi. No. Her shaking turned into a low cackling that turned into a full belly laugh. Her clutching her stomach, was in mirth.

She gasped. "Oh Ben!" She looked at him then. Her eyes glistened with tears from laughter. "You're pulling my leg aren't you!"

He bit his lip, a small smile started at the corners of his mouth as he shook his head no. Her face fell. She saw the moment when he saw the horrified look she felt on her face, mirrored in his eyes.

Slowly she shook her head. A small gasp of denial escaped past her mouth as he nodded.

"Come here love." He gathered her in his arms and rocked her gently as her body wracked with silent sobs.

Good lord... The man I love tells me I'm pregnant, with his child and I laugh in his face. He must... hate me.

Abbi felt crushed as she pulled away from Ben's comforting embrace.

A baby?! But how? I can't be... can I?

She felt like an idiot. The woman was supposed to tell the man.

Her mind raced going over the telltale signs. *How did I not know?* With her past pregnancies she had always known.

Good Lord. I'm 45 soon to be 46. I'm too old to have a baby!!

She needed to escape, to think, to work this out in her mind. She needed to be alone. She needed... to go home.

She got up from the bed and stalked back over to the closet. Yanking the door open, she tossed her belongings over her shoulder onto the bed.

"Abbi! You can't leave," Ben said quietly watching her.

"Watch me," she muttered, stripping off her hospital gown.

Standing naked before the window, she heard Ben exclaim, "*Good God woman!*" As he hurried over to the window to snap the curtains shut.

"Love, they need to monitor your titter levels." He stood there, hands on his hips, head tilted to the side, staring at her belly. "Only for a couple of days."

She snickered, yanking her shirt on over her head. "It's titer levels Ben. And they can do that in Canada."

He reached out a hand to rub her back, stopping himself, instead he quietly said, "Abbi... please."

His tone had her freezing. With one foot in her pant leg, she turned around to face him, her eyes shooting to his.

The look on his face tore at her heart. She dropped her pants in defeat as she sat heavily on the side of the bed. She couldn't do this to him. This was his child too. And truth be told, she was being selfish. As silly as it was; she didn't want to share him with anyone. Aside from all of that she was scared. Scared as hell and wanting to dart out the door back to the safety of her home.

Ben sat beside her. He dared not touch her, knowing how she could at a moment's notice go off and run from him. Never to stop running. The thought terrified him.

"Love. You are the single most important thing in my life. Never doubt that for a minute." He took hold of her shoulders. "I know you're scared; I am too..." He took her hand then and began tracing circles in her palm. "I'm afraid of losing you. I'm also afraid of you walking out that door and never looking back."

Is he nuts?! Yes, I want to run out the door, but never to return to him? No. I will always return to him.

"Ben... I..." He took her face in his hands, guiding his mouth to hers. As one hand slipped to cradle her head, she felt his desperation in that kiss. His fear, his worry, and his love for her. He pulled away, searching her eyes with his fevered ones.

"Abbi, what I'm trying to say is that for me, your health is paramount. I don't want you having my baby if it means I could lose you. That almost happened last night. I'll never take that chance again." Just him uttering those words, was his undoing. His eyes teared up. "You're okay with that right?"

She nodded. Reaching up, she wrapped her arms around his neck. She laid her head against his strong chest as their tears flowed freely.

She needn't have worried. Ben knew her all too well. Or it was his love for her. Deep down she knew what was scaring her, and it wasn't her fear of sharing him. She was carrying a life... their child's life. Ben knew she wouldn't be able to make that decision herself if it came to that. He knew that she could never do it. He was her rock, her light and voice in the storm once again.

A small cough announced someone at the door. "Excuse me...I really need to be taking your blood now."

"Abbi?" Ben whispered.

She nodded, pulling out of his embrace. She slowly got up. The nurse must think she was nuts. Wearing nothing but her shirt, she pulled the blankets back and silently crawled back into bed, pulling the covers up to her chin.

As the nurse came to her side, she bit her lip when she saw the needle. The hand that slipped into hers, lightly traced back and forth. Ben. His ever-soothing touch was always there when she needed it most. She glanced at him giving him a watery smile.

No wonder she had been so emotional lately. Her hormones were through the roof. She gazed at him as she felt the needles sting. Watched the emotions play across his face, the instant empathy he felt for her. If she had ever had any doubts before, in that moment she knew he would be a loving husband to her and wonderful father to their baby.

She made up her mind. No matter what, she would have this baby for him.

Her biggest fear was also her biggest secret, one that he knew nothing about. She had to tell him. She just hoped that they found out who was trying to kill him first...

Chapter 16

Abbi made a beeline for the washroom as she raced down the narrow aisle of the jet. She was having a terrible time going home. Foregoing the long drive, they had decided the quickest way to get back was to fly straight to Toronto and for the first time ever she had to do it sober.

She slammed the door and knelt before the commode, as the wave of nausea turned into her upchucking the contents of her breakfast. The thought of throwing up in a public toilet again, especially one so confined as the airplane, had her retching for a solid ten minutes. She leaned back against the door and prayed that was the end of it.

When she felt it was safe to move, shaking like a leaf, she grabbed hold of the sink and clawed her way to a stand up. She was so incredibly tired, and she needed a drink. Preferably a gin and tonic but the tonic would have to suffice. She splashed water on her face in hopes that would wake her up.

Sighing she took a hard look at her reflection in the mirror and frowned.

Wow, I look old.

Her eyes grew large as she caught in the mirror the reflection of a man materializing behind and heard, '*Well, you have been to hell and back, Abbi. What did you expect?*'

Spinning around, she saw that she was alone. Not only was she tired she was now hallucinating and hearing voices.

She snatched a handful of paper towels in disgust and patted her face dry. She froze as her ring sparkled in the mirror. A sudden fear gripped her chest tightly and it had nothing to do with the plane. Something was wrong, terribly wrong.

KIM LEANED AROUND MARK to look at Ben. "Where is Abbi? We are close to landing; she needs to get back here."

Mark answered. "She ran off to the washroom." He looked across Abbi's empty seat at Ben. "What's taking her so long?"

"I'll go see," Kim said.

"No. It's fine, I'll go get her." Ben got up and slowly maneuvered down the narrow aisle with his cast. He wasn't up to answering any questions from the others. Abbi and he had decided to keep her pregnancy quiet for now... just in case.

"Abbi?" he knocked on the door. "Love, we are close to landing."

Abbi took a steadying breath. She felt so clammy and dammit she was dizzy. Swiping a hand over her face she winced as her hand brushed the wound on her temple. A reminder of what she feared most, the possibility of losing Ben. She cleared her throat. "I... ah. I'm coming." She unlocked the door and pushed it open to see Ben standing there.

He lifted a hand and tucked a stray curl behind her ear. "You okay?" he murmured.

Not wanting him to see the fear in her eyes she nodded and quickly ducked under his arm and headed back to her seat.

As he watched her make her hasty retreat. He knew now wasn't the time to question her about anything.

He made his way to his seat and noticed the grip she had on her armrests as he sat down. He reached to take her hand, to offer her comfort but thought better of it. He smoothed his hand down his pant leg instead.

Neither of them said a word as the plane slowly descended towards the ground. Not wanting to look at her for fear she would bite his head off, Ben sat in stone silence, looking straight ahead. Relief washed over him as he felt her small hand reach for his. Turning his palm up, he clasped hers in a reassuring grip. As the landing gear engaged and the plane taxied down the runway, he risked a glance at her.

She sat there, green to the gills and as beautiful as ever. He brought her hand to his lips and placed a soft kiss on the back of it. She slowly turned, a soft smile on her lips. Which at once turned into horror.

Ripping her hand free of his, Abbi frantically searched for the vomit bag. No matter how many times she swallowed, the bile refused to stay down. There wasn't time to make it to the washroom; passengers were already preparing to disembark. And no vomit bag was in sight. She tore open her purse, stuck her face inside of it and promptly threw up.

"Oooh. Myyy. *GOD*!" Mark yelled, horrified at what he'd just seen. His eyes grew larger by the second as he desperately scrambled backwards, up and over his seat. "What is *wrong* with you Abbi?" He hissed, standing on the seat behind his.

"For cripes sake Abbi. You just threw up in your purse!" Kim said the obvious.

"Mom, are you okay?" Ava asked concern written all over her face.

"Of course, she isn't *okay*, Ava." Mark spit out, tossing a hand towards Abbi. "She just puked in her purse! Who does that?!"

"Enough!" Ben cast a warning glare at the lot of them. "Come on love... lets go home," he murmured, as he took her hand. She followed him down the aisle as the rest of them sat there staring in shock.

Tears stinging her eyes, Abbi was mortified.

I will never fly again...

She didn't care if he wanted to go to England, she would take a ship and meet him there in a month.

"Whoa..." Tim was the first to break the silence. "Is Ben always like that?"

Kim raised a brow. "No, not usually." Something was going on with Abbi and Ben. She knew it, just the vibe she was getting from them. And she was determined to find out.

ONCE INSIDE THE AIRPORT terminal Ben headed straight for the car rental agency.

"Abbi, didn't you say that you drove part way?" He looked at her. "Where is your vehicle?"

She leaned on the counter for support and propped her head in her hand. "I called Lane from Tennessee and asked him to pick it up from the hotel for me."

Abbi watched as he signed two rental agreements. She nodded to the papers on the counter. "Why two?"

He kissed her on the tip of her nose. "Because we are travelling the rest of the way home...alone. But before we head there,

I thought we'd stay a night or two here in Toronto. If you're okay with that?"

As much as she wanted to get back to her own bed, the idea of being alone with just him sounded perfect. Once they were home, there would always be someone around.

She smiled and nodded her agreement.

"Come on. Let's break the news to the others," he said, grinning as he held the door open for her. "Ah... there they are."

Abbi glanced to where he was pointing. Kim and Mark were looking in opposite directions.

Kim turned just as they were approaching them.

"Where the hell did you guys go?" She asked. "We've been looking for ages for you two."

Abbi glanced around. "Where is Ava and Tim?"

"Washroom," Kim said. She was uncomfortable. She wanted to say something but was weighing the reaction her words would have... from Ben.

"Look guys." Mark started. "I'm sorry for my actions back there on the plane." He shrugged and pursed his lips. "I've just never seen anyone..."

Abbi stuck her hands in her back pockets and rocked on the balls of her feet. "Throw up in their purse before?" She grinned at him when she noticed all colour run from his face.

"Yeah... that."

"It was either that or your lap." Abbi smirked.

Mark uncontrollably gagged at the visual.

Ben let out a bark of laughter. "She's got you there, mate."

"I'm sorry too." Kim muttered just as Ava and Tim returned.

"Hey guys," Ava hurriedly said. "Tim was just saying he heard on the news that..." she turned to Tim. "What was her name again?"

"Gwendolyn Pearce," Tim replied.

Ava nodded. "That's right! Anyway, she escaped police custody."

Mark frowned. There weren't too many people he knew with the name Gwendolyn, but he knew at least one. He was about to speak when Ben and Abbi said in unison "Who?"

Tim stepped forward and held his hand out to Ben. "By the way, I'm Tim Steel. We weren't properly introduced with all the hoopla that was happening." Ben took his hand in a firm grip, he still wasn't sure who the guy was, only that he knew Abbi from the past.

Abbi looked between Ava and Tim. "Does someone mind telling us who this Gwendolyn is?" she asked.

Tim sighed as he looked down into her eyes. "She's the one who shot you Abbi. She's Daisy..."

Abbi stood in stony silence. *Is that why I felt something was wrong on the plane?*

Ben scowled. "What do you mean she escaped? How?"

"Well, after you two left for the hospital the place was stormed by every agency possible. The US Marshals, ATF, DEA and FBI. The place was shut down with the sheriff being towed off to jail as well. Anyway. She was locked into the back of a cruiser or so everyone thought. When the officer went back to his car...she was gone. The only sign that she had been there was a silicone mask, her coat and..."

"She couldn't have gotten far?" Kim interrupted. "Not in that cold at least."

"Normally no. What everyone is thinking is that she slipped under the radar. With the disguise that she was wearing, it was simple to do." Tim explained.

Abbi stood there in a daze. *What was the 'and' part Tim didn't finish?* She wasn't the only one to catch that, as she noticed a dark look pass over Ben's face. "And what?" he asked.

"Uh... and a message, written in lipstick on the window..."

Abbi clenched her teeth. "Spit it out Tim. What did the message say?"

"It's not important Abbs."

Tim saw the warning, flash in her eyes. He swallowed hard, taking a step back.

"It said, 'I never leave a job unfinished.' But don't worry, I'm sure she'll be caught soon... hopefully."

Ben took Abbi by the arm. "Come on, let's get out of here." They started walking away when he stopped. Turning around he tossed a set of keys at Mark. "Here, we'll meet you at home in a few days."

"What?!" Kim hurried around them to block their retreat. "Where are you two going?"

"To a hotel. Just for a few days." Ben sighed. Kim of all people should understand that. "We need this time...alone, Kim." He raised his brows to her.

She nodded and said, "Sure, I get it." Now how would she figure out what was going on between them if she couldn't analyze their every move? She threw her arms around her sister. Looking at Ben over Abbi's shoulder she said to him, "Promise me you'll take care of her."

Ben nodded. "You have my word."

Taking a deep breath, Kim ran her hands down Abbi's arms to take her hands in her own and gave them a squeeze.

What the hell is that?!

Her eyes shot to Abbi's left hand. Kim's eyes bugged out of their sockets as she stared at the ring on her sisters' finger. She looked at Ben, a smile on his mouth.

"You didn't even tell us!" Kim cried. She looked at Abbi, her voice coming out in an accusing squeak. "You didn't tell me!"

"With the hospital and all, I never even thought Kim. I'm sorry," Abbi said, tiredly. She was starting to feel the bile burn in throat again.

Abbi glanced at Ben, locking eyes, she sent him a silent message.

"Right." He nodded. "Now you know why we need to be alone; we need to be going now Kim." He chuckled, waggling his eyebrows at her.

She blushed three shades of red. "Of course. You two go and enjoy yourselves. We'll see you in a few days."

As they walked away Abbi promptly stopped and fumbled with her purse.

Kim could be heard excitedly telling the others in a sing/song voice, "We're gonna have a wedding."

If Abbi ever stops throwing up, we will... Ben thought. "Love, let me help you." He held her purse while she once again stuck her face in it. "All good?" He asked, passing her a water bottle.

She shakily nodded and took a sip. "Yeah." She wiped her mouth on her sleeve. "Thank goodness my wallet is in my pocket. I think I need a new purse. No amount of laundry soap is going to get that clean."

Ben chuckled. "Abbi. Don't ever change my love. Come on. Let's go buy you a new purse."

Chapter 17

Abbi flopped onto the hotel bed, sinking deep into its opulence. Ben had gotten them the best suite available. When she protested telling him all she needed was a bed and him, he countered that they would be there a few days and wanted to make the most of it.

A soft satisfied purr came from her throat as she snuggled into the mattress beneath her. She needed a cat nap was all. Just a tiny one, she thought as her eyes drifted shut. She felt the bed sink beside her as Ben laid down next to her. She was too tired to even look at him. She was exhausted from everything.

After the doctor had given her the go ahead to travel it had been a hurried frenzy of activity. Racing to get to the airport, her anxiety had her on high alert for the flight back home. The dreaded trip to the washroom brought a bad taste to her mouth just thinking about it.

"Do you want the fireplace on?" Ben murmured.

Abbi melted at his words. Damn. There it was. That sexy way he had of saying things. *Oh, how I've missed it...*

Abbi bolted upright, wide awake looking straight at the fireplace.

"Oh my God, I knew I saw that man somewhere!"

Ben scrambled to sit beside her. Brushing her hair away from her eyes, he asked, "Are you okay? Please don't throw up on the bed!"

She sat in a daze.

"Abbi?" Ben took her by the arms and turned her towards him. "What is it?"

She snapped her eyes to his. "Ben. I need to tell you something. You're going to think I'm crazy..." She nodded rapidly. "And that's because I likely am."

He laid back against the pillows, motioning for her to come to him. Pulling her close he said, "I won't. I promise. Now, tell me, what is it that has you bothered so?"

"Before we went to you..." She shoved a hand in her hair. "I can't believe I forgot to tell you any of this."

"It's fine. You've been through a lot the last few days." He murmured, resting his chin on her hair.

"True." Taking a deep breath, she began. "We had gone to the crash site. I had to see it for myself..." She looked at him and laid a hand on his chest. "Despite already talking to you and knowing you were gone, I had to make sure you weren't there."

"I'd have done the same thing."

"Good."

He chuckled at her response. Urging her to continue he waited for her to begin.

"After Mark and I came back from... where you had landed, the local police where there. A lot of them, at least five cars. Tim had called them." She shook her head. "Anyway, I was asked to go sit in a police car with an officer. Nice lady... she offered me cookies. I think it was a bribe so I would sign her copy of my book." Abbi frowned. "Which reminds me." Titling her head, she stared at the opposite wall. "... it's still in my purse."

Ben raised his brows, a smile breaking on his lips. "You mean..." A giggle bubbled up from his throat.

She slowly nodded "... Yeah. That one. I'll need to send her a new copy."

"I'll say!" Ben knew that wasn't the end to her story. "Go on, love."

"I realized something was wrong when I saw the look on Mark's face." She looked at him then. "I tore out of the cop car and demanded to know what was going on... Do you know what that creep Sheriff Martin said to me?"

Ben saw red at the mention of the Sheriff's name. He stiffened as his eyes took on a menacing glare. Quickly, he buried his nose in her hair masking the look from Abbi's eyes. He thought back to the last words the two had exchanged. What he wouldn't do to be in his prime physical condition, standing in front of the sheriff now and he say what he had about Abbi then. He would beat the bloody hell out of him.

She backed away and searched his eyes. Laying her hand along his jaw she said, "What's wrong Ben?"

He licked his lips. "Nothing, sweet one. Go on."

He was lying she knew it. Not lying exactly, more so protecting her from something.

"Okay. Well, he said it was an open investigation and he wasn't at the liberty to discuss it. Anyway. I need to get to the point of my story; this stuff is all so trivial now."

Ben chuckled, looking at her he saw the tiredness etched on her face. She was so lovely. He leaned close to her, taking her chin in his hand, he brought his mouth mere inches from hers, "I agree," he whispered, before claiming her lips with his.

Abbi saw stars. This man could melt her in seconds. It was crazy how her body reacted to his touch.

She leaned back to look him in the eyes. "Yes. Um. Well, I tore out of there threatening to leave everyone behind. We raced down the highway. I had no clue where I was going... South was where I was headed, as if drawn to go that way. We ended up in a small town called Martinsville at some creepy looking B&B. The owner opened the door as if she were expecting us." Pausing she scrunched up her forehead. "Come to think of it... she did know. She was expecting us. She called me by name."

"Really?" Ben looked at her curiously.

"Yes. Her name is Hester Riley."

Goosebumps ran up Abbi's spine when she said her name.

Ben leaned over, towards the foot of the bed and grabbed the comforter pulling it over them as he laid back against the pillows.

She sighed in delight at his thoughtfulness.

"So... is that it?" he asked when she said no more.

"Yeah no." She shook her head. "There's more. This is the crazy part..."

Ben looked at her, waiting for her to continue. She smiled at him, taking hold of his hand.

She was stalling he could tell. "Abbi just tell me. I promise I won't think you're nuts." He grinned.

"Fine!" She cleared her throat.

"Abbi," he said, in a sexy, warning growl.

"Okay!! Well, after we were there a few days, I'd sent you a text and was hoping for a response. Mark was sitting on the chair, chatting away. He wanted to know what I had stuffed in my pocket. It was my book." She looked at him. He wasn't following her she could see, needing to explain she said, "The cops' book. Anyway, he went off to bed because I was ignoring him, while I was reading it. There was something bothering me... about it."

"Oh?" Ben squinted at her; his brow furrowed. She reached up to smooth the lines away. It wasn't working...

She waved her hand in dismissal when he kept looking at her. "That's a whole other story that I'm too tired to tell right now."

"Okay." He chuckled. Truth be told he was getting tired too... But he had to wonder if that was why everything seemed so familiar about the time at the farm... Her book.

"So anyway, Hester scared the crap out of me. She had been sitting there the whole time apparently while I was reading." A nervous giggle slipped past her lips.

Ben caught it, knowing exactly what it meant. She was getting scared. He gripped her hand tightly, and traced circles across the back. He sat there silently waiting for her to muster up the courage to go on.

Abbi sucked in a steadying breath. Still not believing what had happened at that old creepy house.

"Hester... She asked me if she could tell me a story. I said sure." Abbi laid her head on his shoulder and shuffled closer. "She told me about the man she fell in love with... and then she told me how to find you. Gave me precise directions. The name of the road. Even what the farm looked like... the smell of it."

A tickle started in her throat causing her to cough. Leaning over him she grabbed a bottle of water from the nightstand. Taking a long swallow, she capped it and tossed it on the bed.

"How?"

"Franklin. Her love. He told her to tell me."

Ben's brows shot up. He'd heard Abbi crying out that name the last night at the farm in his dream. It's what woke him. He shrugged his shoulders. "Why couldn't he just tell you himself?"

"Mhm. One would think he could, right? Wrong...He was killed in the war... he came back to her," Abbi said, curling up beside him.

He leaned back to look at her and asked softly, "He came back to her? As in how, Abbi?"

She didn't answer, instead she placed her chin on his shoulder, and replied, "I didn't believe a word of it, of course. Until...He knew about your note. This one..." She reached into her bra where she kept it close to her heart and handed it to him.

Ben unfolded the paper. He knew what was on that note. He had written it countless of times. Whenever he flew, he'd write it over again, tucking it into his seat. He read it anyway... One moonlit night...

He held it up. "Did anyone else know about this?"

Not that I'm having doubts about her story, but one of the others had mentioned it maybe.

"Mark was there. He found it but didn't read it until after he handed it to me."

"Right. It's not likely something Mark would talk about anyhow. Especially to a stranger, an odd one at that by the sounds of it." He sighed.

"That isn't what convinced me," Abbi said. "I mean I thought the same as you; someone mentioning it. But no."

Ben looked at her and searched her eyes. "Then what did?"

"Franklin said I had to hurry...you didn't have much time."

A tear slipped from the corner of Abbi's eye. Ben laid a hand along her neck, his thumb rested lightly in front of her ear. Holding the side of her face, he watched it as it trailed down her soft cheek. He leaned forward and caught it with his tongue. He ran his thumb along her jaw, stopping to rest it just below her bottom lip. Gently he lifted her chin, bringing his face within inches of hers.

He was going to kiss her. Abbi knew it, she yearned for it...welcomed it. But first she had to finish telling him. "He knew what I wanted for Christmas, Ben."

He pulled back, still holding her in his arms. Shock registered on his handsome face.

He searched Abbi's face for a reaction, looking deeply into her eyes, he asked, "You told no one?"

She shook her head no. "I swear, I didn't breathe a word of it to anyone. Only you."

He laid back against the pillows, pulling her with him.

Abbi laid there with her head on his chest, listening to the steady beat of his heart. She could feel his hand drawing circles across her back. He was lost in his own thoughts, she knew that.

He either thinks I need to be locked up or he's coming up with a logical explanation...

"Love. You didn't answer me before. Tell me. You said Franklin came back to her... He came back to her as in how?"

"As in a ghost, Ben." She tilted her head up to look at him. "He also came to me in the washroom on the plane. I thought I had recognized him. When you mentioned the fireplace, it came to me...Hester had pictures of them together on her mantel." She laid her head back down. "You don't believe me, do you?"

It was a ghost. It was Franklin that had visited me. Waking me...but why?

"Yes, I do Abbi. Tell me. Was he clean cut in one of the photos? About 24 years old?"

She snapped her head up. "Yes... How do you know?"

He caught a stray curl, twirling the silkiness between his fingers. "Because the night you came, and I had decided to leave. I woke to you crying the name Franklin in my ear... he was in the corner of my room. He told me, not out loud but in my mind, that it was time to go. He was wearing his uniform, Abbi..."

A misty chill overcame the room just then. Instantly they were both off the bed, bounding into the living area of the suite.

"What shall we do?" Ben smacked his hands together.

"I don't know but I'm getting outta here," Abbi said, heading for the door to get her shoes on. She snagged both, her new purse, and the bag it came in on the way... just in case the urge to vomit struck again.

Chapter 18

Ben chuckled and caught her by the hand before she could dart out the door. "Come here," he said silkily, twirling her towards him. "How 'bout dinner and a movie in instead?" She landed hard against the length of him. Her eyes growing large as his arousal pressed against her.

He searched her face for any signs of pain that the impact of hitting him so hard could have caused.

"Are you okay?"

"Lord, yes!" she said breathlessly.

He smiled and murmured, "I love you Abbi; no ghost is stopping us." He growled as he dipped his head to capture her mouth. He kissed her the way he had so desperately been dreaming about since being reunited.

She dropped her purse and the bag on the floor, moaning as she wrapped her arms around his neck. She opened her mouth in response to his seeking tongue.

Ben grabbed the back of her thighs and hiked her up as she wrapped her legs around his waist. Never breaking contact with her sweet mouth, he carried her to the sofa. Laying her gently on it, he covered her face in soft kisses. Running his tongue along her jaw to her ear.

She sighed in pure delight when his teeth lightly grazed the sensitive skin there. It had been so long since he held her in his arms like this. Abbi couldn't get enough of him, his touch, his mouth, his scent all made her dizzy with wanting. She leaned her head back, arching her neck to his seeking lips that caused her insides to liquefy. The need to feel his skin against hers was driving her up a wall. Tugging on his shirt she pulled it up over his stomach, her hands brushing against the hard ripples of his stomach. She felt exhilarated when his muscles reacted to her touch.

Grinding his arousal against her, he nearly passed out from the pain it caused in his leg. It was in the way. He couldn't stay in this position any longer, half on the sofa half off.

Panting, Ben groaned out. "Abbi..."

His voice drunk with passion, caused her nerve endings to hum all the way to her core. Cold air met her as his heat moved away from her. She opened her eyes. Something was wrong.

"Ben! What is it? Is it Franklin?"

"What? No. God no. It's my leg." He grimaced with pain. "I'm sorry love. It's locking up on me." He felt like a piece of shit, doing that to her. She had been ready to fly out the door and he'd stopped her. Now their night was ruined, more ways than one.

"Honey don't be silly. You have nothing to be sorry for." She kissed him then. Taking his breath away with just her lips.

"Let me get your crutches." She jumped off the sofa in search of them, returning a short time later. "You should be using them all the time you know. Here. Let's get you into the shower." She sent him a sly smile. "My new puke bag will cover your leg perfectly. I'll order some food. Chinese sound good to you?" she asked, looking at him.

He nodded. "Sounds perfect but will you be able to hold that down?"

"Never know until I try! I'll order it while you get un-dressed." She guided him into the bathroom to a padded bench that sat alongside the wall near the tub.

Stating the obvious, Ben said, "Um...there's no shower in here."

Abbi whipped out her cellphone and called room service. "A bath it is." She walked over to the massive tub and turned it on as she gave their order. Sitting her phone on the vanity, she turned to Ben.

"Why are you still dressed?" She said, grabbing his pant leg.

He grinned. "I am, I was too busy watching the ravishing vision before me."

Chuckling, she tugged on his pant leg. "Were you now?"

"Mhm. You know..." He waited for her to look at him. Jerk-ing his chin, he said, "That tub is big enough for the both of us." He sent her a sexy grin. "And I could use a hand. You know, to hold my leg up...or something."

She managed to get his pants of. But decided not to take the boot off, she didn't want to hurt him anymore than he al-ready was.

Abbi put a hand on each of his knees, pushing his legs apart she stood between them. Leaning down, she lightly traced his lips with the tip of her tongue.

"One step ahead of you handsome." She smiled against his mouth, as she shimmied out of her pants.

Reaching for the hem of her shirt she pulled it off in one fluid motion followed by her bra. She gasped as his tongue flicked out, lapping at her nipples. His hands went around, squeezing her butt, drawing her towards him as he sucked one then the other.

Good lord. Abbi wasn't expecting the sensations his mouth caused within her body and was close to fainting. She knew what he did to her, but this was different, more heightened, more exhilarating.

She held tight to his head. Knowing any second, she was going to go off like a rocket. She had to take control now and get him in the tub. She moaned as his fingers slipped under the leg of her panties and inside her. That was it, that's all it took. Leaning her forehead against his, she clenched every muscle in her body in response to his touch, shaking uncontrollably. *I've never had an orgasm while standing before.*

She dropped her forehead to his shoulder and opened her eyes, looking directly at his erection. Problem was, he still had his underwear on.

She slowly brought her head up, lifting her eyes to his. She could see the fevered passion in them. Abbi grabbed his boxers by the waist and said, "Lift up."

He did so silently, knowing exactly what she was thinking.

Pulling them off him, she slid her panties to the floor then straddled his legs. Holding onto his shoulders she slowly settled herself in his lap. Looking each other in the eye, Abbi could see the concern flood his.

Would it hurt her this way, or the baby?

Knowing it would go deep, he had to ask her. "Are you sure love?"

Biting her lip, she nodded as she placed her knees on the seat, either side of him and slowly lowered herself onto his shaft. Ben couldn't help the hissing that emitted past his lips as her wet warmth enveloped him. Somehow, she wrapped her legs around him, drawing him in as deep as she could. He wanted nothing more than to grab her by the hips and ram into her softness, but he held back. She had to be the one to control this.

Ben took hold of the back of her neck and brought her to him. His lips sought out the spot behind her ear. He knew it drove her crazy when he touched her there. Flicking his tongue along her ear, his voice thick with passion he groaned, "For the love of god Abbi, if it hurts you, stop. Because I can't."

In response she held him tight as his mouth devoured hers, she slowly rode him, quickening the pace when his hands cradled her back. Trusting him, she leaned against his strength while his mouth suckled at one breast than the other. Holding his head to her, she could feel him coming ever closer to his release. Increasing the pace, she clenched him with every stroke until as one, they both shuddered in spent pleasure.

They held each other afterwards, both lost in their own thoughts.

Ben was blown away, as usual. Every time they made love, she always amazed him.

Why the hell do I leave her for months on end... just to film a movie?

He knew he said it before and yes maybe he was having second thoughts about quitting acting. But this, this that just happened between them? Hell no, he wasn't leaving her again. He never wanted to miss a second of his life with her.

"Are you okay?" He murmured, looking down at her.

"Yeah. Sorry," she mumbled. "I'm getting up," She took a deep breath and untangled herself from him. Not wanting to leave his arms, she turned quickly to the tub and wiped her eyes, hoping Ben wouldn't see her tears.

The water was close to overflowing she bent down to shut the taps off and lifted the lever. She waited to gain her composure as the level slowly lowered. She heard Ben hobble over to her side then felt his lips softly touch her shoulder.

"What's wrong?"

The tone of his voice had her tearing up again.

How can he read me so easily?

Was she really that transparent? She liked to think she wasn't.

Abbi took a shaky breath. She might as well tell him. It was time she revealed her secret.

Methodically, she lowered the lever, plugging the tub. Turning, she looked him in the eyes. The strength she felt in his gaze gave her the courage to tell him.

The look of fear in Abbi's eyes had him scared as she ran her hands through her hair, and said, "Ben. I'm terrified..."

"Of what?"

"Of everything."

He raised a hand to touch her. "Abbi, you have no reason to be."

Shrugging off his hand, she darted behind him and stalked to the door. Grabbing a hotel robe from the hook, she slipped her arms in and tied the sash tightly at her waist.

"I do. I'm sick with worry knowing that crazy bitch is on the loose. I'm scared that whoever put her up to this will never be found..." She stopped.

Ben watched as she stood there, not more than five feet from him. He studied her face.

I couldn't be more in love with her if I tried...

She looked at him then. Her soft gray eyes changed like storm clouds gathering on the horizon as she violently started to shake.

"What is it?!" He pleaded.

Abbi bit her bottom lip, trying desperately to stop its quivering. She didn't want to say it. "I...I don't know if I can have our baby Ben..." She covered her face as her tears ran down her cheeks, the memories from days gone by flashed through her mind.

"What? Why?" He went to her then. "Love, you can tell me. Just say it."

"I...when I told you before about my ex. It was all true. We had been slowly drifting apart for years. There was no longer any love between us when we ended it. I was in love with him, when the kids were small, I won't deny it... but. He killed that when I lost the baby."

Baby?

Ben stood a little taller and inhaled sharply. "I see." He couldn't help being affected by what she just said. He felt like such an ass. His heart went out to her and yet he couldn't help but feel jealousy because she had loved another.

"No, you don't! I was far into my pregnancy. He blamed me! Said it was my fault! My fault that *his* child had died, like it wasn't mine too." She sobbed. "Do you have any idea what it's like to carry a child? A child that you know will never take a breath on its own, to full term?!" She started to pace. It wasn't Ben's fault her ex was a first-class asshole. She shook her head sadly. "Of course, you don't." Quietly she continued. "I had to deliver my baby... alone. With no one there to lean on, no shoulder to cry on. He wasn't even there for the funeral. He just swept it all under the rug as if it never happened."

Ben didn't say a word as he pulled her into his arms, stroking her back as her sobs wracked his soul.

How could any man act so... Heinous to the woman he loved?

"Abbi, I promise you, I'm not your ex."

She leaned back, looking at him with her tear-stained face, her eyes puffy from crying.

"Ben, I know you're not. But..." She swallowed hard. "If the same thing happens this time, and who knows with my age. I couldn't bear it. I'm more terrified of losing you, of you blaming me, than I am of any risk to my health."

"Love. It will never happen. I promise you." He lifted her chin with his hand. "I will be there every step of the way. If history repeats itself, I'll never leave your side. As a matter of fact, I promise you'll have to beat me off with a stick." He smiled softly. "And even then, I would never leave you," he murmured. As light as a feather, he brushed his lips against hers.

Leaning back, she looked at him in awe.

What did I ever do to deserve this beautiful man?

Softly she returned his kiss as her tears flowed freely. *Good lord will I ever stop crying around him?*

Honestly, she didn't care, she would cry the rest of her life if it meant she could always have him. Someone up there must have known she needed him in her life. Whoever it was she silently thanked them.

Chapter 19

They were on their way home after a blissful three day stay in Toronto. Ben had wined and dined her, they went shopping, and sightseeing and both were ready to go home.

He had insisted he could drive. His right leg was perfectly fine he'd told Abbi. They had an hours' worth of driving left to get to Pearl Lake and he was starting to feel the effects of being cramped up. He hated to admit it, but he couldn't finish the drive. He had to switch with Abbi. Taking his eyes off the road for a second, he glanced her way. She was leaning back in her seat. Her arm bent at the elbow, rested on the door with her head propped in her hand. Staring at him.

"What?" He laughed looking back at the road. Licking his lips, he said, "Tell me. How long have you been watching me?"

"For the last twenty minutes or so."

"Oh yeah...?" He cocked an eyebrow and sent her a suggestive smile. "Do you see anything you like?" A sexy smile flitted on his mouth as he took her free hand, bringing it to brush it against his lips.

"Always," she responded in a throaty purr. "So...When are you going to pull over so I can drive?"

"You can tell, can't you?" He looked at her. She just nodded. "Right. The next town we'll switch."

"Fine, but if you need to stop sooner, we can pull in someone's driveway." She suggested, looking out her window.

It had snowed since she'd been away. When she'd left home in search of Ben, the fall colours were out in full force. She couldn't believe she'd been away for nearly a month.

Her birthday was in less than two weeks, a month before Christmas. She wanted nothing for either day.

I have everything I want right here in the car she thought sleepily as her eyes grew heavy. She fought the urge to rest them as the scenery sped by.

Abbi awoke with a jerk from the vibration of her phone coming from her pocket. Fumbling with it, she answered with a tired, "Hello?"

"Mom?! It's Ava. Where are you guys?"

Abbi noticed the panic in her voice. Bile rose in her throat as she was instantly taken back to the day Ava raced into her house to tell her of the plane crash.

She hit the Bluetooth button on the cars' display, connecting her phone to the speakers. She thought it silly of Ben to link it to a rental but now was thankful he did.

"Ava, honey, slow down. What's wrong?"

"You need to get home right now. Someone shot Brutus with an arrow."

Ben stepped on the gas. There was no time to stop now.

Abbi felt her world spin out of control. Not Brutus, her dumb sweet hero.

"What happened, Ava?" Ben asked.

"I don't know. We let the dogs out about an hour ago. Molly and Lucy came back." Her sniffling came through the speakers. "They wouldn't come in. They kept barking and running away. Mark said they looked like they wanted us to follow, so we did. We're at Mack's right now, him and Doc are working on him."

"We'll be there in about a half hour. Stay put at Mack's. We will meet you there," Ben told her.

"Mom? I'm so sorry," Ava cried into the phone.

Ben glanced at Abbi. She was sitting there clutching the phone in her hand, staring straight ahead, as tears streamed down her face.

"Ava, your mom can't talk right now." He reached over and took the phone from Abbi. "We'll be there in twenty minutes." He disconnected the call and frowned in thought.

Ever since I came into Abbi's life, I've brought her nothing but pain.

"Love?" He looked at her again. The look she turned on him sent a ripple of dread over him.

Is she thinking the same thing?

"We'll be there soon. Are you okay?"

"Yeah." She nodded.

"What is it?" He was afraid to ask but he had to. "Please. What are you thinking?"

She looked at him blankly. "What am I thinking?" Her mind raced. All that kept running through it was this was all too familiar. Too familiar because she wrote it.

Someone was after them; and they were getting it all from the Jasper Killings...

Abbi whipped her head to look at Ben. She put a hand on his arm.

"Tell me, you should know. Does this not all feel eerily familiar to you?" She raised her brows expectantly at him.

He gave a slight nod. "Yeah, a bit. Why? What are you thinking?" He asked, driving up the hill that would bring them into the village of Pearl Lake.

Frustrated, Abbi groaned.

It was there, she knew it! But for the life of her she couldn't put her finger on it. When she was back at Hester's house reading the bit about the train crash, she felt it then too. She shook her head. She must be having brain fog from the pregnancy. She needed to read her book from beginning to end, but first she had to get to Brutus.

Ben pulled the car to a stop outside of Mack's store. Abbi scurried out in a flurry. Glancing back, she saw Ben struggling to get out of the driver's seat.

Racing to his side, she opened the back door and took his crutches, holding them impatiently while he maneuvered out the door.

"Thanks. Sorry for that. Go!" He mumbled his apology; he knew she ached to get to her dog.

She instantly felt like a bitch. Wiping the frown from her face she gave him a watery, tired smile.

"You have nothing to be sorry for Ben. Come on." Despite wanting to race to the back door of the store, she kept his pace. She held onto his waist, so he didn't slip on the snow and ice until the last five feet, then she let go and hurried inside.

It took a second for her eyes to adjust from the blinding snow. When they did, she saw Brutus was lying on his side; a white bandage was wrapped around his middle. When he saw her, he whined, raised his head, and cried at the sight of her.

"Oh, my poor baby." She rushed to him. "Stay Brutus. Lay down." She crooned softly to him as she hugged him tight.

"Ben." Doc nodded.

"Hi. How is he doing?" Ben came to the side of the table and leaned down, his face next to Brutus. The dog thumped his tail and turned, giving him a sloppy kiss.

"He'll survive. The arrow missed everything vital. He might have a bit of nerve pain in the future. Time will tell," Doc said to them as Mack came into the back room.

"Ben, Abbi!" Mack boomed. "So good to see you two again. I hear there is a big surprise soon. Congratulations!" Mack smiled.

They both looked up at Mack at the exact same time. Confusion and shock on their faces.

"Surprise?" Ben raised his brows at Abbi. A 'who did you tell about the baby?' look crossed his face.

She shook her head, silently conveying she didn't.

"Yeah." Confused over their reactions, Mack motioned to the front of the store. "Ava said you two were getting married."

Both felt relief when they realized their secret was safe.

"Right, right! Yes. Abbi said yes," Ben nodded, grinning.

How did we both forget that?

Abbi looked up in surprise. "Ava is here?"

"Yeah, she's manning the store while we tended to Brutus here," Mack said to her.

"Ben, could you?"

He could tell she was fighting a battle; wanting to stay by Brutus' side and going to see Ava.

"Of course, love. Go. I'll stay with him."

Abbi bent to give her dog a kiss on the head then left in search of her daughter.

Ben turned his attention on Doc and Mack. He knew something was up but didn't want Abbi to know... at least not yet.

"Now that she's out of the room." Ben cast his eyes between the two men. "Will one of you tell me what the hell happened to him?"

Mack gave a heavy sigh. "It was no accident, Ben. Someone deliberately shot him."

Squinting, Ben asked, "How are you so certain that it was done on purpose?"

Doc opened a drawer. "Here." He passed the feather end of a broken arrow to Ben.

"Turn it over Ben," Doc said, grimly.

Ben scanned the surface as he turned the aluminum arrow with his fingers. He frowned. There was writing scratched on its surface. He traced the words with his thumb... 'Hollywood... you're next'. Ben tapped it against his hand, testing the weight of it. "Who else knows about this? What's written on it?" he asked.

Both men shook their heads. "Just us Ben, and whoever wrote it," Mack answered.

Ben nodded, a scowl on his face. "Let's keep it that way please. Abbi doesn't need to know."

He had a feeling he knew who was behind it. He just needed to prove it.

Chapter 20

"Did you send the warning like I told you?" The caller asked.

"Of course, I did... I told you I had it in me." She blanched at the memory. The dogs yelp, searing through her mind, would stay with her a long time.

"Excellent! Now, lay low."

"Wait! Are you going to tell me who you are and who is behind all of this?" she asked.

"I'll contact you in a few days with further instructions." An audible click was heard.

She looked at the phone in her hand. "What a bastard," she muttered to herself. "Lay low?! In this God forsaken town?" The man was pure evil...

BEN WATCHED FROM THE door as Mark carried Brutus into the bedroom.

"Here, Mark. Lay him down here," Abbi said, tossing a pillow aside for him to lay Brutus on the bed. She crawled up beside the dog and put her head on his chest.

"You two go, we'll be okay now, won't we buddy?" She crooned, smoothing her hand down the dogs back.

"Sure thing. We will be in the kitchen if you need anything, just yell," Ben said, covering her with a blanket before following Mark out the room.

Once in the kitchen Mark went to the fridge and grabbed two beers. "I stocked your fridge for you," he said, popping the caps on both, he passed one to Ben.

Ben took it, looked down at the bottle in his hand and said, "This wasn't a random act, Mark. It wasn't a hunter who accidentally shot Brutus. This was on purpose. Whether they were aiming for him or one of the other two, I'm not sure, but it was a warning." He pulled the head of the arrow from his back pocket and placed it on the counter.

Mark looked down at it and frowned. "This is it?" He raised inquisitive eyes to Ben. Seeing him nod, Mark picked it up and examined it.

He read the message carved in the arrow. "Do you remember that actress I dated a year ago?" Mark asked, studying the feathers.

A snort came from Ben's direction. "Which one?"

Never taking his eyes off the arrowhead, Mark grinned. Barely above a whisper, he answered. "The brunette."

There had been a few brunettes if Ben's memory served him. "Briefly." He shrugged. "Wait, was it her you were with at that restaurant in France?" Ben squinted.

"Yeah, that's the one. The only time you met her." Mark paused. Looking up from the arrow, he looked Ben in the eye. "I really thought she was the one. I thought I wanted to marry her. I was a fool."

Ben leaned against the counter and crossed his arms. "Why? I thought you two had hit it off rather good."

"Yeah... so did I. That was until she saw you that night. After that she had made you her mission."

Ben looked at him in disbelief. "That's insane Mark. I've never met the woman outside of that day." Ben saw the look on Mark's face. "Man. I'm sorry, I had no clue. Not that it would have mattered if I had known." Ben trailed off.

Mark waved a hand. "I know you didn't." He laughed. "Believe me. It was for the best. Luckily, I dodged the bullet with that one. If I had known she was capable of something so... so repulsive... I... Thank God, I broke it off."

Ben raised a brow. "Where are you going with this Mark?"

Mark held up the arrow. "This. I'm going with this. That girl I dated was a champion archer, she was known as The Piercer. She could pick the dimple off a gourd fifty feet away..."

"A... Gourd? What the hell does a gourd have to do with all this? And what does *she* have to do with it?"

Mark sighed then took a swallow of his beer and looked at his friend. "Her real name was Gwendolyn Heed. She changed it to Pearce... for acting purposes."

Ben rubbed his jaw. Dawning flashed in his eyes as he pieced the puzzle of Mark's words together. "The Piercer... She's Gwendolyn Pearce. Otherwise known as... Sonofabitch! She's Daisy..."

"That night at the farm I wasn't paying attention to her. Even in her disguise I likely could have picked her out in a line-up. Is there any way you can get a hold of the agents who were there?" Mark asked.

"You mean Smitty and Dean. I suppose I could try."

"You could try the local department back in Tennessee, but they didn't seem to know too much of anything," Mark said.

Ben hobbled over to the coat rack. "I think I stuffed one of their cards in my jacket," he said. As he stuffed his hand in one of the pockets, the doorbell suddenly chimed above his head, he stopped and looked up at it.

"Are you going to just stare at it or open the door?" Mark asked.

"Yeah, I am," Ben said. As he pulled his hand free, he looked down to see that he held Dean's card. Pulling the door open he was shocked to see the man standing in the flesh.

"Well, it's about damn time." Came that unmistakable drawl of Dean.

He stood there leaning against the wall, a half grin on his face as Smitty walked up behind him.

"How...?! I was just going to call you," Ben stated. Stepping back, he held the door open for them to enter.

"Were you now? I guess we beat you to it," Dean said. Taking off his sunglasses he folded them and stuffed them into his pocket as he took in his surroundings.

Mark reached into the fridge and produced two more beers. He handed each of them one. "What are you two doing here?" He asked.

"Thanks, my man. Cheers." Dean tipped back the bottle taking a long swallow.

"We have reason to believe that Gwendolyn Pearce is headed this way. She was spotted at the border," Smitty said, looking at Ben. "Ah... Unfortunately, we didn't have a photo of her without a disguise to alert them before she slipped through."

Ben frowned. "How long ago was this?"

"Day before yesterday," Dean answered.

A hushed silence fell over the room as Abbi could be heard calling Ben from the bedroom.

"Excuse me," he muttered. As he headed to the hallway he stopped and turned around. "Don't any of you tell her what's going on."

"Ben, she has a right to know..." Mark said as the two cops nodded their agreement.

"Not a word. I'll tell her myself." *When the time is ready*, he thought as he turned down the hallway to go to her.

Mark looked at both men. "Sorry about him. He's been a bit off since... well everything. So, are you two staying in Pearl Lake or something?"

"Yeah, if we can find lodgings. Is there a motel around here?" Smitty asked.

"Nope, everything closes up for the winter. Well, there is the cabins, but they aren't heated. You would freeze come morning. This place is big enough, but I can't speak for Ben and Abbi." Mark nodded towards the window. "You could always stay over at my place on the sofas."

"Might just take you up on the offer," Dean said. "We need to stay close by in case she decides to show up. Staying in the car out front isn't a choice."

Mark held up a finger. "Ah, about that." He marched over to the counter where the arrow laid. "This was in Abbi's dog. I think it was Gwendolyn who shot him."

Dean looked at him, taking the arrow in his hand. "You don't say?"

"What makes you think that Mark?" Smitty asked, whipping out a small notepad and pen.

"I dated her last year. She's a marksman in archery. Plus, she had the hots for Ben."

"If she was interested in him, then why go after him?" Dean raised his brows.

"Wait... She never acted like she even knew him, and he had no clue who she was. She took her disguise off in front of him. I was there," Smitty said, pointing to his chest.

"That's just it, she's an actress, a convincing one at that. The whole time we dated she told me she wanted him. They met once, very briefly in a restaurant we were dining in," Mark sighed. "And... you guys didn't know this, but Ben had amnesia while there. Whatever it is, she's a first-class bitch."

"Amnesia huh?" Smitty looked thoughtful. "So, is it fair to say that she really isn't after Ben... but Abbi?"

Mark sighed. "I think she's after both... Why else would she shoot the dog and write that?" He pointed to the warning on the arrow.

Frowning, Smitty took the arrow and nodded. "Good point..."

Taking a swig from his bottle, Dean nodded. "Ah... we'll take you up on your offer Mark."

"HEY, MY SWEET."

Abbi smiled as Ben laid down behind Brutus. He gazed at her over the dog's head as he stretched out a hand to catch one of her silky curls.

He whispered, "How is he?"

As he thumped his tail against Ben's leg, Brutus looked up at him and gave a sloppy kiss across Ben's face.

"Better." Abbi grinned. "I thought I heard voices?"

"Yeah, you did." He twirled the strand between his fingers, marveling at the softness. "Dean and Smitty are here. They're in the kitchen talking to Mark."

Ben saw the concern flash across her face. "Oh? Did they say why they came?"

Of course, she would ask... What the hell do I tell her?

"Ah... Well. Maybe. You called for me before that was discussed." God, he hated lying to her but he felt he didn't have a choice.

"Okay." She pushed herself up to a sitting position. "I guess I should get up."

Ben reached for her hand. "Are you sure love? I mean..." He trailed off when she sent him a look.

Giggling, Abbi said, "Yeah... I'm sure. Besides. Brutus needs to go out, I think. He's been letting off some godawful farts."

Ben laughed. "Yup, I'll say that he needs to then." He moved to the edge of the bed. Putting his arms under Brutus, he slowly raised him off the bed.

"Good Lord, put him down. I'll call for Mark," Abbi told him, scurrying on the bed to help if the need arose.

"It's fine. I can get him. The leg is already feeling better." He lied of course. But he needed her to come with him, having her hear about Gwendolyn wouldn't do. "Just open the doors for me, will you?"

She jumped off the bed and crossed the room to the French doors. Pushing them wide, she followed Ben to the yard as he gently placed Brutus on the ground, panting from the exertion.

Abbi searched his face. "You're overdoing it Ben."

"No, I'm fine." He looked towards the lake. "Just need to catch my.... Sonofabitch!!"

Brutus let out a low warning growl.

"What?!" Abbi cried in confusion. Following his line of view, horror filled her face.

"Get in the house Abbi. *Now!*"

She didn't listen, she ran towards it. It wasn't the fact that the dock was on fire. No. It was the fact that a publicity poster of the Jasper Killings was in the middle of the inferno on a wooden sign and written across it, were four words... 'YOU ARE NEXT ABBI'.

Chapter 21

It was December 1st. It had been less than two weeks since the dock fire and one week since Abbi's birthday. Everyone had come with birthday wishes. Kim had baked a cake and Luke and Lane had called promising to be there for Christmas.

She said no presents and threatened to throw them in the lake if someone went against her wishes. It didn't matter that the lake was frozen, she swore she would cut a hole in the ice and shove them in if she had to. Ben had wanted to take her to the city, but she had insisted the time they had spent in Toronto was her birthday present.

Brutus was well on the mend. His strength was returning steadily, no longer needing to be carried to do his business in the yard. Ben's cast was off. His leg still hurt from time to time but had healed nicely and Abbi was over her morning sickness. The only thing hanging over their heads was the fact that Smitty and Dean were staying between their house and Mark's. There was no sign of Gwendolyn, not since the fire. Even then, they weren't entirely sure it was her. Just Mark speculating.

Ben was currently sitting at the table pouring over the Jasper Killings. Abbi thought there was a connection somehow to it. She'd marked pages here and there and he would go over them with a fine-toothed comb. Nothing stood out to him. Sure, there were a couple of similarities, but that could be all coincidence.

Wait a minute...

Abbi dragged a box into the room. Standing up, she sent a glance at Ben. He was engrossed in the book.

"You want something to drink?" she asked. Looking at him on her way to the fridge, she noticed he was frowning.

Slowly he got up and walked towards her, the book in his hands. "Say, Abbi. What did you mean by this part?" He asked turning to gaze at her as he cradled the book in his hands.

The look he sent her way would never get old to her. His green eyes sparkled with curiosity; his brow furrowed. His lips.... *My goodness he looks hot!*

She took the book from him and looked to where he pointed. She read the part twice, each time it didn't register. All she could think of was jumping him.

Good Lord Abbi... get a grip!

It'd been so long; she'd forgotten what pregnancy did to a woman's libido and she rather liked it.

"Um..." She looked up at him and bit her lip. "I, ah. I'm not sure honestly."

He raised a brow at her and sighed. "Really?" He asked in amazement. "You wrote it? How can you not be sure?"

"It was a long time ago. I don't remember."

He sighed and scratched his head. "Right... okay." He motioned to the box she'd left in the middle of the room. "So... what's in the that?"

She smiled. "That would be Christmas decorations. I thought we could put them up."

Grinning, he pulled her into his arms, bringing her up tight against him. "Yeah? What about a tree, is it in there too?"

She linked her hands behind his neck and leaned close, her mouth inches from his. Slowly she shook her head. "We have to cut one down."

Abbi heard the quick intake of his breath as she brushed her lips against his and was shocked at how quickly she felt his arousal against her.

Ben's lips caressed along her jaw, slowly he made his way to her ear as he ground his hips into hers and murmured, "When did you want to do it?"

She inwardly groaned. Abbi caught the innuendo.

She wanted nothing more than to strip him where he stood and jump his bones; but they were losing light. If she wanted to get the tree up and decorated before midnight, they had to get it now.

She pulled back and looked deeply into his eyes.

"Right now." She tugged his hand.

Ben eagerly followed her. Confused as to why she was leading him into the garage, he said, "This is kinda kinky, and I love it." His eyes sparkled when she turned the light on, a grin on his face. "But don't you think it's a bit cold out here?"

Instead of answering. She marched over to the peg board that held the tools on the wall and grabbed the axe.

Abbi passed it to him.

Looking up through her lashes with a soft smile on her lips, she said, "I promise. I'll make it up to you... after the tree is in the house and it's decorated."

He raised his brows and let out a low hiss. "You're a tease, you know that don't you?"

"I do, sorry. Now let's get going, were losing light." She laughed as they headed into the house to get their winter gear on.

THEY HAD BEEN WALKING for a few minutes looking for the perfect tree. Abbi was chattering on, telling him what she wanted. One large enough that could be cut in half. Why she wouldn't just want two trees was beyond Ben. But he didn't question her motives.

He was thinking back to the night he'd been alone in a forest just like this, nothing but trees and snow around for miles. The only thing keeping him sane was the woman that was now at his side.

He hadn't really thought much about it since that last night at the farm. But now, being here he realized how easily he could have died that night. Good thing Smitty and Dean had found him when they did.

Funny how neither of them knew at the time that they were both law enforcement. Dean was a convincing actor that was for sure.

Wait a minute...

Ben stopped dead in his tracks.

Walking with her head down, Abbi was concentrating on stepping in Ben's tracks in the deep snow while she pulled a sled behind her. Not seeing him stop, she landed on her bottom squarely on the sled.

Ben whipped around. "Oh shit. Abbi are you alright?" He bent down to give her hand up. "The baby? Is it okay?"

"As long as I'm not carrying her in my butt, I'm sure she's fine." Abbi laughed and took his hand.

Tugging her to her feet, he looked taken aback. "Her? What makes you think it's a girl?"

"Just a feeling." She smiled. "Don't worry, she could be a boy."

"I just never really thought about the sex of it." He kissed her on the nose. "It doesn't matter to me what the baby is. As long as it's mother is healthy."

"Sweet talker." Grinning, Abbi pointed, and said, "There, that's the one."

He turned around, looking up to see a tree at least 15 feet tall.

"Of course, it is," he said, dryly.

Ben caught her as she threw her arms around his neck and planted the most sensual kiss on his lips he'd ever felt in his life. He was ready to take her on the snow right there when she handed him the axe. "Chop, chop." She winked and smiled as she smacked his ass.

"Woman." He growled. "You're doing this on purpose aren't you?" He grunted taking a swing at the tree.

"Of course!" Abbi giggled. "I need to get you all hot and bothered for later."

She walked around as he chopped at the tree. Looking for the perfect garland she'd said.

Which was perfect for him to think about Dean. It dawned on Ben before Abbi walked into him that Dean might not be who he said he was. Was he really a US Marshal like he claimed or was he like Gwendolyn, a washed-up actor, turned killer for hire?

And what was it that made Abbi think there was a connection to her book? That was still eluding him. He'd gone over every section she had marked off. Was he reading too much into it? Was the answer right there before his eyes? Maybe it had nothing to do with the book... but the movie?

He stopped for a second. Starting to work up a sweat, he took his coat off and dropped it on the ground. *Wait a second...*

"Hey, you were there when Dean and Smitty came to the house, did you hear...?" He turned in the direction she went off in. "Abbi?" Dropping the axe, he followed her tracks until he heard her crying. She was kneeling on the ground looking into the trees. He went down beside her and turned to see what was upsetting her so. Ben couldn't believe what he was seeing. There in the trees was the soft hazy glow of Franklin, with a woman at his side. Ben licked his lips, without taking his eyes off the sight before them, he asked, "Is that....?"

Abbi nodded, as the tears ran down her face. "Yes Ben, it's Hester." He pulled her into his arms as the two apparitions disappeared into the trees as one.

"Please, don't cry Abbi, they're together at last," he said, trying his best to soothe her.

She clung to his sweater. "I know Ben. I wanted to bring her up here for Christmas. She was so lonely in that big ugly house. She had no one, not even a cat."

"I know, love. Come on. I'm just about done chopping the tree down." He pulled her up beside him and walked her back to the clearing.

"Why don't you go back to the house, and I'll finish here?" He suggested. "You're freezing."

She shook her head. "No, I'm fine. I'll wait." The temperature was dropping now; she could see her breath. She wasn't leaving him alone out here.

"Okay. At least throw my coat over you," he said. Picking it up off the ground, he shook the snow from it and draped it over her shoulders.

She stuck her arms in the sleeves, not for herself, but to warm it for him. They still had a fair walk back to the house.

"One more hit Abbi and that'll be it." He grinned, picking up the axe. "Do I yell timber or something?"

She chuckled. "If you like."

"I do!" He took one hard whack at it with the axe and with a yell any lumberjack would be proud, yelled "Timber!!"

He draped an arm around her shoulders. "How was that?" he murmured as he nuzzled her neck. Leaning back, he looked at her for approval.

"It was perfect. You're perfect." She kissed him. Clinging to his lips, she softly said, "Let's go home."

As they walked back to the house hand in hand, big fat snowflakes fell silently as the house came into view.

Ben looked at her as he pulled the tree into the garage. "Are you tired?"

"Surprisingly, no. Besides... we have unfinished business."

"Right! You get the stands, and I'll chop this baby in half." He rubbed his hands together in anticipation.

She wagged her finger at him. "Don't forget. We have to decorate them... tonight."

He sighed. "I know, I know."

Tomorrow would be soon enough to figure out Dean's role in all of this. Tonight, was for them...

Chapter 22

The living room looked like a Christmas card, with the twinkling lights, and a fire in the hearth.

Abbi sipped her hot chocolate as Ben put the last ornament on the tree; he had some skills she had to admit. He had done so well trimming the bottom half, that it looked like a full tree. The top half was already sitting on a table, decorated, in their bedroom.

He walked over to her and took the mug out of her hands. Placing it on the coffee table, he sat on the couch and pulled her onto his lap and said, "So, what do you think?"

She shivered. "It looks fantastic."

"Are you still cold?" he asked, noticing her red nose as he rubbed his hand down her arm.

She got up to throw another log on the fire, then came back to sit at his side. Laying her head against his arm, she said, "A little, yeah." She turned her head to look at him. "Are you tired?"

Ben took her hand and linked their fingers.

"Are you?" He looked at her. He groaned when he saw her eyes filled with desire.

Abbi shook her head no. Wordlessly, she slowly climbed onto his thighs and settled herself on his lap. Ben thrust his hands in her hair, cupping her head, he brought her mouth to his in a crushing kiss.

She grabbed the hem of her shirt and tore it over her head. She needed to feel him against her bare skin. Her breast felt heavy and full straining against her bra, needing to be released.

Ben could feel her tugging on his shirt as he ran his hands over her back; she felt like ice.

Tearing his mouth away, he took hold of her hands and searched her eyes. "Are you feeling alright?"

She tugged on his shirt again, trying desperately to rip it off him. "Of course. I'm fine."

"You're freezing, Abbi!" He took her by the hips and set her aside. Grabbing the throw off the arm of the couch, he wrapped it around her so only her head poked out. "Wait here. I'll be back for you."

Picking up her mug, she watched as he took off down the hall. Truth be told, she was incredibly tired. But that wasn't going to stop her from making love to him. She hoped...Her luck she'd fall asleep in the middle of it. This pregnancy was certainly kicking her in the ass. She couldn't remember being this tired, teary eyed, or sick with the other two.

Ben went back into the living room; he saw a smile tugging on her lips as she stared at the tree. She looked so beautiful sitting there in the soft lights. He wished he had a way to read her mind.

Abbi looked at him. A grin played on his handsome face as he advanced towards her.

"No, no, no," she chanted, squealing with laughter. She held her hands up to keep him back. "Don't you dare!"

He didn't listen. He scooped her up in his arms despite her protest. Abbi had no choice but to wrap her arms around his neck.

"Not over my shoulder. I'll carry you proper," he said. Taking care to treat her as the fragile angel that she was, he gently kissed her on the lips.

"It's bath time," he murmured against her mouth.

He could feel the thrilling shiver run through her body at his tone. He knew it would. Every. Single. Time.

How can I get so worked up over his voice for God's sake? It's not just the pregnancy either. It's him.

Abbi glanced around the dimly lit bathroom. Candles flickered their soft glow, a hint of jasmine hung in the steamy air. As he kissed her, he let her legs go; she clung to him as her body slid along his hardness.

He deepened the kiss, while his hands worked the button of her jeans. Slowly he unzipped them sliding them down along with her panties over her hips.

She cried out when he took a step back.

"Just a second," he murmured, taking his shirt off.

He gazed at her as she stood before him in only her bra. Removing his jeans, he kicked them out of the way. Reaching out, he hooked a finger into each shoulder strap, slowly tugging them down her arms as he kissed her forehead.

Her breath quickened when his lips blazed a trail to her ear. His tongue flicked to that sensitive spot.

He's going to drive me mad, she thought as he dragged his mouth to her earlobe and bit it gently.

Abbi was no longer cold. In fact, she was on fire. She was so mesmerized by what he was doing with his mouth she didn't feel when he unsnapped the front of her bra. But there she was, standing, in all her glory, guiding his head to her breast.

She melted as he took one nipple into his mouth, while his fingers worked the other. She felt like ripping his hair out as his mouth lowered as he kneeled before her, his fingers trailing down her chest to her belly leaving a trail of goosebumps behind.

Ben laid a hand on the soft swell of her belly. His eyes stung with tears at the thought that his baby was nestled within. Ever so tenderly, he placed his lips there. He kissed her stomach and silently promised the baby within it would be cherished, just like it's mother.

His actions touched Abbi so much, that she felt the lump of unshed tears in her throat. She pulled Ben up to her, wrapping her arms around him. He took her thigh and hiked her up against his arousal.

She wrapped her leg around him, as he did the same to her other thigh. His hands splayed across her bottom, his mouth devoured hers, as he carried her to the waiting bath.

Just for this purpose, when they had built this bathroom, they had the hindsight to put it half sunken into the floor.

Not wanting to drop her, he set her down on the floor and held her hand while she gingerly stepped into the tub, sinking up to her neck. Abbi sighed in delight as the warm water lapped over her cold skin. But it didn't match the fire Ben had ignited within her. She wanted to reciprocate. She reached for his legs as he stepped in the water before he could sit. She pulled him close to her.

He looked down at her, saw the mischievous grin, the glint in her eyes.

"Love..." he growled out as she touched him with her lips. She didn't do it often, and he never asked her to...but bloody hell he loved it when she did!

He about lost it when her tongue ran along the tip of his cock. "Abbi...!" he hissed a warning. She needed to stop now if he was going to be of any use to her. As much as he loved her mouth on him, he loved being inside her more.

She leaned back, looked up at him innocently. "What?"

Ben lowered himself into the tub, sinking down, he pulled her into his arms.

His voice dripping with desire, he smiled. "You know exactly 'what', you little vixen."

She stifled a yawn. "You have room to talk."

"Am I boring you that much?" He laughed.

"Not at all. I'm just thinking, if you want to finish what we started, we should be heading into the bedroom. Otherwise, I might pass out after and drown."

He sat there a moment, squinting in thought. Suddenly, he nodded and said, "Right. Let's go." He pulled on her hand as he stood up.

Abbi laughed hysterically at his eagerness as they ran naked and wet to their adjoining bedroom.

She collapsed onto the foot of the bed, her legs hanging over the edge. Expecting any second for him to join her.

Where the hell did he go?

She was too lazy to move. "Ben?"

In answer, she felt his hand on her leg.

She looked down the length of her body. There he was kneeling on the floor, a mischievous grin on his face.

"Oh my..." She was in for it now.

She shivered as his lips touched her ankle, trailing up to her knee and then her thigh. She wrapped her leg around his shoulders, urging him forward.

He was mere inches from her heat, and it was pure torture waiting for his mouth to descend to her most private core. She cried out as his lips, moved to her other leg, trailing down to her ankle. She felt like grabbing fistfuls of his hair and yanking him to her. Mashing his face into...

Good Lord where did that come from? It was so unladylike. *I can't do that...can I?*

Hell yes, she could! She pulled his head towards her. Whimpering she pleaded with him, "Ben... please!"

His throaty laugh was hot against her skin as his tongue flicked out to taste her. A soft moan escaped past her lips as she wrapped her legs around his shoulders. That was all the encouragement he needed. He teased and suckled with his tongue as she writhed beneath him. If she squeezed her legs any tighter, he feared his head would pop. But still, he pleasured her, drank from her like she was the elixir for his soul. Now that he thought about is, she really was. She was his life.

Abbi couldn't take it any longer, she needed him inside her and now. Pulling him up, she wrapped her legs around his waist. Slowly, he eased into her. Reveling at how her warmth encompassed him. He could feel the tremors from within, telling him she'd already climaxed, and she was going to again; very soon.

Ben slowly withdrew, taking his time. He loved watching the emotions play over her face.

Abbi thrust her hips up to meet him, a rhythm they had perfected long ago. She knew he was close, as was she. She also knew he was worried about going too deep. He really needn't be afraid. She stopped.

A panicked frown flashed across his face as he gazed into her eyes. "Abbi, what is it? Did I hurt you?"

"Not at all." She flipped onto her stomach, brought her knees up under and backed towards him.

"We can't do it this way!"

She looked at him over her shoulder. "Trust me... we can, and we are. Come on, you'll see." She kissed him and felt him melt beneath her touch.

Bending forward she brought him with her. Hesitantly, he entered her softness once again. He so desperately wanted to stop, to tell her he wasn't doing it this way...but he couldn't. Gently he pushed onward through her silken folds until he was buried deep within her.

She purred as he swelled inside her and moaned when he moved. Matching her stroke for stroke... they both cried out in a frenzy of pleasure before collapsing into a quivering heap.

Chapter 23

Ben brushed his lips across Abbi's brow as he slowly eased his arm out from under her. It was morning and she was still sound asleep. He quietly got dressed, watching her the whole time to make sure she stayed that way. He had some business to take care of that she didn't need to know about.

Opening the door, he was greeted by all three dogs looking expectantly at him; Molly was gearing up to bark her excitement at seeing him. Quickly he closed the door, taking care not to bang it shut. With a soft thud, he took her collar in his hand.

"Shhh girl." He guided her down the hall. "Come on guys. Let's get you outside," he said, as they trotted on his heels to the back door.

It had snowed overnight, Abbi and his tracks completely covered from last night. He watched as Brutus and Molly raced to the edge of the frozen lake. Looking down, he opened the door to let Lucy back in. Ben picked her up and dried her paws off, he glanced out the window to check on the others as he did so, when something caught his eye. He frowned.

Our tracks are covered...so whose are those?

Just then his phone started ringing. Taking it out of his pocket, he saw it was Mark. Juggling Lucy and his phone he answered it with a quick, "Yeah?"

"Thank God you're up," Mark said.

Ben frowned, setting Lucy on the floor. "Yeah, what's wrong?"

"You need to get over here man, like right now. Kim is having a fit. She's freaking out." Mark lowered his voice to a hushed whisper. "She thinks that one of the cops is a spy."

Huh... clearly, I'm not the only one who thinks it.

"I'll be right over," Ben said, hanging up. He called the dogs in, quickly fed them, the cats and Bird, then put his coat and boots on. Leaving a note for Abbi he headed out the door.

The sun was blinding off the new fallen snow when Ben stepped out the door. Twenty feet from the house he stopped and glanced down at the single set of footprints. It was hard to judge from the size of them if they were a man or a woman's, whoever it was, they had no business on his land. He followed them to Mark's yard, where they suddenly disappeared into the brush.

Mark was right, Kim was freaking out. He could hear her shouting clear across the yard. Making his way up the steps, he stopped as the door flung open.

Quickly he ducked, as two suitcases were tossed out, just narrowly missing his head. "Bloody hell Kim!" he shouted.

"Will you get in here now," Kim hissed. She ushered him inside as her eyes darted around the yard.

Ben raised his brows. "What is wrong with you?!"

"Me?!" Kim huffed. "There is nothing wrong with me. Now get the hell in here before they pick you off."

Ben shook his head in disbelief as he crossed the threshold. He jumped when she slammed the door shut and sent her a brooding look.

Ben glanced around the room as he shucked his winter gear. Ava and Tim were sitting at the table. Mark was leaning against the breakfast counter. Dean and Smitty were nowhere in sight.

"Thanks for coming." Mark grabbed a mug. "Do you want a coffee?"

"Ah sure." Ben nodded. Looking at Kim, he took a seat at the counter. "What's going on with Dean and Smitty?"

She shrugged and started to clear the counter. "Oh, nothing much. Just that one or both are spies," she spat out.

Mark sat the mug in front of Ben. Muttering out the side of his mouth while he poured the coffee, he said, "See man, I told you."

Nodding his thanks to Mark, Ben asked Kim, "What makes you say that?"

"Cuz she's nuts," Ava mumbled, as she scanned the contents of the Jasper Killings.

Kim shot her a sour look. She turned her attention back to Ben. "Well, for starters they sneak around, watching constantly." She jerked a thumb at the table. "Tim said the other day, Dean was rooting around in the garbage looking for evidence."

She nodded self-satisfied. Finally, someone was listening to her.

Ben squinted and looked at her. "What makes you think it was evidence?" He folded his arms across his chest. "I mean, maybe he dropped something in there and was looking for it?" He raised his brows and leaned forward, looking around Kim to Tim at the table. Tim silently mouthed his agreement. Ben nodded and straightened to look back at Kim.

She was scowling at him. "Yeah...? Yes, well maybe he didn't. Maybe, he's in cahoots with whoever shot Brutus. I mean, just this morning I saw him over at your place. Peering in the windows."

Stonily, Ben looked at her. "What?" He blinked. "What time was this?"

Kim visibly gulped. When Ben looked at her like that or anyone else for that matter, it meant trouble. Abbi would kill her if he did something to Dean.

"Ah... well, you know maybe it wasn't him," she squeaked. "You know, it likely wasn't. My eyes aren't all that great." Turning to the table, she said, "Ava. Didn't I just say last week that I needed my eyes checked?"

Ava looked up from the book and shook her head. "Nope."

Kim's eyes grew large as she gritted her teeth and made a fist at Ava. Spinning on her heel she looked back at Ben. "It might have been a..." She stammered, her mind racing... "moose! Yeah, now that I think of..."

"Kiiiim..." Ben ground out the warning.

Damn it! She hated when he used that tone on her.

"Okay!" She cried, wringing her hands. "Yes, it was him. He was scurrying around like a rat in search of crumbs, the sneak." She marched up to Ben and stuck her index finger in his face. "If you do anything to him... I'll.... Abbi will kill me." She stepped back as he stood up, towering over her.

Ben weighed her words in contemplation.

She was right, Abbi would kill them both. He nodded his agreement. "Alright. What time did this happen Kim?"

"Fine!!" She finally gave in. "It was early. The moon was still out, but I could clearly see that it was him. Plus, I went and looked to see if he was on the couch... he wasn't."

What the hell was Dean doing that early in the morning? Was it before or after Abbi and me...?

"Does anyone know what time it started snowing." Ben glanced around the room, and added, "And when it stopped?"

"It started around 11:00 I think," Tim said.

"I got up around 3:00 and it wasn't snowing then," Mark replied. "Why, what are you thinking?"

Ben was about to answer when they heard stomping feet on the porch. Someone was coming in. He stalked to the door and yanked it open. His breath froze in his chest. There Abbi stood, looking like the proverbial snow queen.

"Holy crap!" Abbi exclaimed, jumping. She caught the worried look on Ben's face just before it was replaced with a grin and a glimmer in his eyes.

Something was wrong.

"Morning love." He dropped a hurried kiss on her mouth, took her by the hand, quickly pulled her into the house, and slammed the door shut behind her.

"Hey guys," she said. Taking her coat off she hung it on the coat rack and rubbed her hands together. "What's up?" She asked, looking from one guilty face to the other.

Kim giggled nervously, shifting her eyes about. "What makes you think something is up?" she asked, nonchalantly as she leaned against the counter.

Mark poured her a cup of coffee and slid a plate of cookies on the counter.

Abbi grabbed one and munched on it. She looked at Kim and said, "Because you all look like I interrupted something."

"Oh, for cripes sake." Ava shoved her chair back as she stood up.

Ben shot her a warning look.

"What?! She has a right to know! Mom, Kim thinks Dean or Smitty is a spy for some mastermind, that's out to get you or Ben or both of you."

Abbi turned to look at Ben. "How long were you planning on not telling me this time?"

Ben gazed at her. She could read him so well. Guilt, shame, and fear stared back at her. But there was something more. A fire was burning in him. One of pure hatred. It wasn't for her, she knew. But something else.

He cleared his throat, taking her hand he said, "Abbi, you're not to get involved with this..." When she went to interrupt, he said, "I mean it. This isn't your fight. I've had my suspicions about Dean for some time now. Back at the farm..." Ben thought back to his first meeting with him. He had a feeling Dean wouldn't have hesitated to put a bullet in his brain given the chance.

He sighed. "Anyway. It doesn't matter; I'll take care of it."

"Ben, you're not alone in this," Tim said. "I think I speak for both Mark and myself when I say this. We have your back man."

"What?!" Mark barked in shock. Recovering quickly, he said, "Oh, ah. Yeah, sure thing." He sent his newfound friend a wink and added, "Tim. I'll be right behind you buddy."

"Well now that's settled." Kim clapped her hands and grinned. "When are you two planning the wedding?"

"Right now, Kim," Ben said. "You ladies get a head start. Us three, have a little business to take care of."

Abbi couldn't take her eyes off him as her sister and daughter steered her into the living room. She was terrified of what he was going to do, she just wished she could stop him...

Chapter 24

Abbi tried to pay attention to Ava and Kim as they tossed ideas around about the wedding, she really did but her eyes were constantly drawn to the windows. The guys had bundled up and were out there, looking for what, she wasn't sure they even knew. She presumed Dean and Smitty but was certain neither man was a spy. Too many officers had known them back at the farm in Tennessee. She had to agree that Dean didn't act like a police officer, but it didn't mean he wasn't.

Not paying any heed to Kim and Ava's chattering, Abbi slowly got up from the chair she'd been sitting on. Something was out there across the lake. After living in the house for years, looking out those very windows everyday she knew when something was out of place. She turned and went to the old curio cabinet and opened the lower doors. The binoculars she'd left there when she moved, were gone.

"Guys where did the stuff go that was in here?"

"What are you looking for Mom?"

"My binoculars... I left them when I moved in with Ben." Abbi went to the windows again. She was relieved to see that whatever it was hadn't moved.

"Oh, hang on, I'll go grab them."

"What is it Abbi?" Kim came to stand beside her.

"There's something across the lake." Abbi pointed. "See it?"

"Huh...I do. What is it?"

"I can't make it out, but it almost looks like a tent maybe."

"Here mom." Ava held out the binocular case as she came into the room.

Abbi quickly removed them then raised them to her eyes. She saw a tent, smoke... and a person.

Abbi saw Gwendolyn Pearce looking across the lake, directly in the direction of Ben, Tim, and Mark.

"There she is..." Abbi hissed.

"Who?! Let me see!" Kim said.

"That bitch, Gwendolyn." Abbi pushed the binoculars in Kim's hands as she headed towards the kitchen. Grabbing her coat from the rack, she snagged a set of keys from the counter and took off out the front door.

Hot on her heels, Kim said, "Where the hell are you going?!" She stuffed her feet into her boots and grabbed her coat, she stopped on the front porch. "Sonofabitch she's going after her. Ava, get out here *now*!!"

Abbi ran through the snow to the cars. With no idea which vehicle the keys were for, she pushed the unlock button on the key fob, Marks's truck lights flashed in response. She hit the remote start and the engine came to life with a throaty rumble. Yanking the door open she jumped up into the seat as Kim and Ava hopped in. Sticking the key in the ignition, she threw the gearshift into reverse. She fully intended on backing out, but the truck had other ideas... it stalled.

Looking down in confusion, she saw there were three pedals.

Frustrated, Abbi cried out, "What the hell is this?!"

"It's a stick Abbi," Kim muttered.

"I know it's a stick, Kim!" she shot back. "What's it doing in this truck!"

"Here, push that pedal in and hold it down. No. Not that one! The one on the left." Abbi did what she was told. "Now start it. I'll shift." Once again, the engine came to life. Kim grabbed the shifter and grinded the gears.

"You know... we could just take my jeep." Ava held up her keys, shaking them.

POPPING HIS HEAD UP, Mark whispered, "Was that my truck?"

Ben cocked his head. "Not likely mate..."

"Shush..." Mark strained to listen.

The three of them were laying on their stomachs in the snow, watching Dean and Smitty argue over something down by the lake.

"Nah man. Seriously, I don't hear a thing." Ben mumbled, as he stretched his neck. It was killing him lying in that position. He rolled onto his back and took his cell phone from his pocket.

"It is my truck!!" Mark spat. Jumping up, he turned and took off towards the house as if he were in a race for his life.

"Why do you suppose his truck is running?" Tim asked. He glanced over at Ben and noticed he was frowning at his phone.

Ten missed calls?! Abbi! God the baby! Without a word, Ben scrambled up in a flurry of snow and took off after Mark.

Tim shrugged and turned his attention back to the two down by the lake. Something was going to happen any second; he could just about taste it.

Ben ran around the corner of the house and took in the scene before him, his eyes scanned the area until they found Abbi. She was sitting in the driver's seat of Mark's truck, no worse for wear.

"Get out of my truck Abbi!" Mark yelled. His eyes were bulging as he stood in front of it; his hands spread wide on the hood, intent on stopping it if the need arose.

Ben walked to the side of the truck and opened the driver's door. "What are you doing Abbi?" Reaching in he turned the truck off before Mark had a conniption.

He passed the keys over his shoulder, knowing full well Mark would snatch them up.

"Give me them! Don't you ever do that again, Abbi!" Mark's voice cracked as if he were about to cry. "I could hear the gears grinding down by the lake."

Abbi pushed Ben out of the way. "Come on, Ava," she called over her shoulder as she climbed down from the truck.

"Abbi! Where are you going?" Ben reached out and caught her hand.

Kim stepped forward. "She won't tell us. She took off out the door. Lucky for Mark she can't drive a stick."

Abbi stopped and turned abruptly. "I'm going after Gwendolyn, Ben. And you're not stopping me."

Many times, he'd backed down when Abbi put her mind to something. This wasn't going to be one of those times.

"Where is she?" He looked at her, with the same amount of stubbornness. She stood there looking at him. He grabbed her by the arms. "Abbi. Where the hell is, she?!" He shouted and instantly regretted it. He dropped his hands when he saw the hurt in her eyes. The sting of not what he said but how he said it.

"Love. I'm sorry." He shoved his hands in his hair. "But I can't allow you to go on some wild goose chase."

He knew they had agreed not to tell anyone about the pregnancy just yet, but he didn't care. The woman he loved, who carried his baby was about to do something drastic and he was damned if he'd just stand there and not say something.

Taking a deep breath, he looked deeply in her eyes. "If you're not going to think about your own life, then at least think of our baby's."

Abbi stiffened; her eyes blazed with a fire from within.

Oh shit... I shouldn't have said that.

"What did you just say?" Abbi's voice dripped with steel.

"Oh. My. God!" Kim hopped around to Abbi's side. "You're pregnant?!?" She grabbed her sister by the arms. "I knew something was up!" She yanked Abbi into her arms for a hug.

"What?!" Ava paled. "I'm going to have a little sister. How?"

Recovered from his ordeal, Mark stared at Ava. "Do you really need to ask that Ava?" He then smacked Ben on the back, and said, "Congratulations, man." Turning his charm on Abbi, he took her hand in his and kissed the back of it. "Sweets, you're glowing already."

Abbi squinted at him. *Is he nuts?*

Ben needed to do some back pedaling and quick. "That's not a glow Mark. She's pissed at me."

"Oh. Well, then. Glad it's you and not me," Mark muttered. As he walked away, he put an arm around Kim and Ava, guiding them towards the house. "Ladies. Let's go into the house shall we and have a celebratory drink?"

Stopping in her tracks Ava walked up to Abbi. "Mom, are you okay?"

Oh, my dear sweet girl. Always concerned for me. Abbi shot her a watery smile and pulled her into her arms. Hugging her, she said, "Yes, baby girl, I'm fine. Go with the others. I need to talk to Ben."

Letting Ben sweat, Abbi watched her walk away and into the house before she turned her eyes to him. She could not believe he broke their agreement. She figured he'd have a hard time keeping it quiet but to blurt it out like that, was something she wouldn't forget.

"Abbi..."

Trying desperately to swallow the tears that stung her throat. She held up a hand. "Don't. Please," she whispered. "I can't lose you. Don't you understand that, Ben?"

He looked down at the ground. Glancing up, he pointed to his chest and said, "What makes you think *I* can lose you? You think all I worry about is the baby?" When she was about to interrupt, he said, "No. Don't deny it. I see it in your eyes! Abbi, I would go mad if I lost you. Why can't *you* understand *that*?"

She didn't say a word, she just stood there with tears silently rolling down her cheeks. He wanted to take her in his arms and soothe the hurt away, but she had to make that call, not him.

"Given the chance, Gwendolyn wouldn't hesitate to shoot you again. And I'm sorry I broke our agreement. I shouldn't have mentioned the baby, not in front of everyone like that."

He couldn't help himself. He stepped forward and brushed a stray hair from her eyes. "I never told you this, but you were the only reason I never did anything back there in Tennessee. I knew if I had, I would have been killed." He leaned his forehead against hers. "I couldn't bear the thought of never seeing you again. Touching you again. Never being able to tell you I loved you one more time."

Abbi knew it wasn't just the baby he was thinking of. She knew the strength it took him to not do anything at the farm. He never was the type of person to stand down. She threw her arms around him. God, she loved this man more than life itself and try as she might, she couldn't stay angry at him. She leaned back, searching his eyes, she laid her hand on his face. "I love you more than anything in this world... but don't you ever yell at me again. Got it?" she said quietly.

He grinned. "I'm sorry. I was desperate." Sobering, he said, "I promise love. I'll never yell, shout, or scream at you again for as long as I live. Truce?"

She smiled and nodded. "Yes, truce," she whispered against his lips.

Tim came running up to them as if the hounds of hell were in hot pursuit. He bent over and sucked in a deep breath. "Guys, Call 911. Dean's been shot."

"What? There were no gunshots. By whom?" Ben asked, whipping out his cell phone. He tossed it to Abbi.

It had to be Gwendolyn...

"Silencer...Smitty. He just took off across the lake on foot."

Chapter 25

"*Smitty*?" Ben looked at Tim, shocked. "Why would Smitty shoot Dean?"

"I don't know man; I just know what I saw. And that was Smitty holding a gun on Dean. Shot him right where he stood." Tim shook his head in disbelief as he straightened. He looked at Abbi. "Did you call 911?"

She nodded. "Yeah."

"Good." Tim pulled out his own cell and dialed a number. Putting it to his ear, he said, "Both of you, get in the house and stay away from the windows."

"We can't just leave Dean there to die," Abbi said. "We have to try and help him."

Ben steered her towards the house. "Go. Tell the others. I'll go with Tim and grab him."

Abbi nodded, watching them walk away. Knowing if she didn't leave at that moment, she never would. Turning to go into the house, she stopped, and back at him. "Ben? I love you."

He stopped and looked at her. The look on her face said it all.

Silently he held his arms wide open. That was all the encouragement she needed. She ran to him. Throwing herself into his embrace, she kissed his neck softly and said, "Please come back to me."

"I will Abbi." He brushed his lips against hers and blinked at the sting of tears. "I love you too." He cleared his throat. "Now go, get in the house where it's safe, please."

He stood there until she was inside. He looked at Tim and nodded. "I'm ready."

They stayed along the cover of the tree line at the edge of the property, when Tim held up a hand, signaling Ben to stop. Their next steps would be out along the beach, out in the open making them easy targets. Both men scanned the frozen expanse. Smitty must have made it across as there was no open water that would show he'd fallen through.

"What's across the lake?" Tim asked.

"Ah, nothing really. Just trees and brush," Ben said, as he looked across. "Huh...There is something there I see. Looks like a tent or something."

"We won't worry about that for now. Come on. Let's get Dean and get out of here. Stay low." Tim led the way to Dean's side. He didn't look too good, but he was breathing, and awake and mad as hell.

"That fucking asshole shot me in the goddamn leg!" He seethed. "Help me up, will you."

Ben grinned down at him. "Not such a nice feeling being helpless, now, is it?"

"Yeah. Don't even say it. This is my karma."

Clasping Dean's forearm to hoist him up, Ben's grin turned into a scowl. "Ah, do you mind telling me why the hell you were snooping around my house this morning?"

"Never mind that for now," Tim said. "We have to get to the cover of those trees."

Dean groaned as they guided him back to the tree line. Leaning his back against a tree, he looked at Ben. "I wasn't snooping. I was watching Smitty looking through your windows." He motioned to the spot where he'd been laying not a minute before. "The bastard shot me when I asked him about it."

"Sit on the ground a minute Dean." Tim ordered. Unzipping his coat, he looked at Ben. "Do you think it was left behind by someone. The tent that is?" Taking his belt off he squatted beside Dean and wrapped it around his leg, tightening it as a makeshift tourniquet.

Dean hissed as he felt his leg go numb. As the two men pulled him upright from his spot on the ground again, he asked, "Who the hell would sleep in a tent in this weather?"

Ben shrugged as he and Tim wrapped an arm around Dean's waist, supporting his weight. "It's possible I guess, or it could be a hunter. Whoever it is, they're trespassing. After what happened with Raven, Abbi bought the land up."

The two looked at Ben in confusion as they crossed the back yard. Dean spoke first. "What the hell happened with a bird?"

Ben chuckled as they made their way up the back steps. "Raven Black is a man, not a bird." Ben jerked his head to the corner of the porch. "Get that chair will you Tim?"

Tim grabbed the chair, and together they dumped Dean in it. "He's an actor that got pissed that I was cast in the lead role for the Jasper Killings...." He stopped talking to look at Tim. "Wait a minute. You and Abbi went to school together, right?"

"Yeah. From kindergarten right up until she quit." Tim frowned. "Why?"

"Then you know who Raven is... He went to school with you two. His name was Roland Eddy."

"Roland Eddy, hell yeah I remember him." Tim chuckled.

Ben turned the door handle, only to find it was locked.

"Right. Well, he caused a plethora of shit a few months back. Almost succeeded in killing me and tried to win Abbi over. I beat the hell out of him. Thought I would end up in jail along with him but luckily that didn't happen." Ben sighed. "If it wasn't for him being locked up, I'd suspect he was behind all of this."

Tim's eyes widen in thought. "Hell, Ben I remember that now. It was all through the police departments province wide..."

Ben raised his hand to pound on the glass, but Tim's words stopped him from following through.

His eyes shut to the pain he was feeling, Dean spoke up. "Yeah man. States side too. He made bail just before, and I quote every news source out there, 'Hollywood's most sought actor, Ben Everett's plane has crashed.'"

Something clicked in Ben's brain at Dean's words.

"Sonofabitch." He muttered. "No wonder I couldn't shake the feeling back at the farm that everything was so familiar. My God, it was right before my eyes the whole bloody time." He tossed a hand towards Dean. "I thought it was you!"

"What? Me? What are you talking about?"

Tim was peering in the windows. "Uh, guys... why isn't anyone coming to the door?"

Ben turned and looked too. Something was wrong. Four people in the house and not one of them was watching out for them? He was sure they all would have been glued to the windows. He cupped his hands around his face to get a better look, past the living room into the kitchen; a feeling of dread came over him. His family was in there and something was terribly wrong. Then he saw it... "Someone is laying on the floor."

Dean half rose from his spot on the chair. "What? Who?"

Ben shook his head. "I don't know. But I'm going to find out."

He walked over to the planter in the corner of the porch, lifted it up and took a key from underneath. Passing by Dean and Tim, Ben flew down the steps and crossed the yard to the garden shed. He then took a rock from the garden and smashed at the lock until it fell to the ground in pieces.

"What is he doing?" Tim asked.

"Hell, if I know," Dean said as he folded his arms across his chest as Ben made his way back to the porch.

Tim looked at what he held in his hand. "What're you doing with that axe Ben?"

Ben looked at him. With deadly determination he made his way to the French doors off Abbi's old bedroom. Tim helped Dean hobble along as they followed him.

Silently, Ben fitted the key into the lock. When he heard the click, he looked back at them both. "I'm going to put it in Raven's back if he's touched Abbi."

Dean and Tim looked at each other, slowly they looked at Ben as if he'd gone mad.

Dean scratched his beard. "Raven? Ah, buddy, what makes you think he's even here?"

"Oh, he's here all right," Ben mumbled and jerked his chin towards Dean. "He's the one that shot you."

Dean grabbed him by the arm. "How do you know?"

"Because. Everyone called me by my stage name, Ben Everett, including you back at the farm. The whole time there, only two people mentioned my real last name, Quinn, and the reason for that is because they already knew who I was."

Tim let out a low whistle. "Daisy and Smitty."

"Right." Ben agreed.

"Hold up," Dean said.

Ben turned around. With a cocked brow, he asked, "Now what?"

Dean and Tim looked to one another and nodded. Simultaneously they removed their pistols from their holsters and unlocked the safety.

Dean gave a quick jerk of his head. "Okay. Now let's go."

Ben slowly pushed on the unlocked door. Whisper soft, it opened and the three silently entered the house.

Chapter 26

In the dining area, Abbi, Kim, and Ava were sitting on the floor. Kim was rocking back and forth, and Ava was softly crying as Smitty stalked around the kitchen with a hand to his temple; the other held a gun.

Abbi was glaring at Gwendolyn who stood guard by the front door, she wished she had a hammer to pound that heartless bitch's foot with. The foot that had just kicked her in the stomach. Maybe then she would feel the kind of pain Abbi was currently feeling. She laid her hand over the spot, praying it hadn't hurt the baby.

"What are you going to do with him?" Gwendolyn asked, jerking her chin toward Mark's still form laying by the counter. Blood pooled from the gash on his head onto the floor; caused by the butt of Smitty's gun.

Smitty stopped and cast a deadly look in her direction. He wanted to put a bullet between her eyes for kicking Abbi the way she had. Resisting the urge to raise his gun, he shoved his hands into his hair. "Will you just shut up and let me think a minute," he screamed.

He hadn't meant to hit Mark, he thought it was Ben coming in from the living room. That prick. Taking Abbi away from him. He had planned on doing much worse to Ben when he got his hands on him. But when he'd seen it was Mark who fell to the ground. He didn't know what to do. His plans were all shot to hell.

Smitty's face was itching him like crazy. Rubbing his jawline, he paced back and forth like a caged animal.

The plane crash was the perfect idea. But oh no, Ben Quinn was not an easy kill.

You should have learned that from the last time... the voice said to him.

No. I should have killed him in the States. But no... Tennessee has the death penalty. It had to be done here. It would never do to be dead; I'd never get to be with Abbi then.

Kim looked at Smitty. She was watching him since he'd thrust his hands in his hair. She blinked in amazement when she watched as it slid sideways.

What the hell?! He's wearing a wig!

Try as she might, she couldn't tear her eyes from the sight of it. She knew she would have to bite her tongue from laughing when it slipped clear off his head.

"What the hell are you looking at?" Smitty sneered. "You want to say something to me?" he yelled out, spitting at her.

It was on the tip of Kim's tongue to say a madman when she felt Abbi shift against her. Silently conveying to her to keep her mouth shut. Instead, she forcibly turned her gaze towards the darkened hallway. Seeing the shadow of a man, she silently prayed whoever it was had a gun.

Smitty cackled. "Yeah. I didn't think so."

Abbi looked at him, stalking the room like a crazed man, picking at his jaw. Her eyes widened as she saw his face crumbling where he was picking it. She froze as he stopped and looked directly at her, taking deliberate steps towards where she sat on the floor.

Desperately, she inched back against the chair behind her and squeezed her eyes shut, turning her face away as he reached out to touch her hair. Instead, he dropped his hand and held it out to her.

"Abbi, come with me," Smitty said.

Immediately she was transported back in time a few months. When she'd had the BBQ in this very back yard. She heard that voice before. It was Raven's. She eyes snapped open.

"No..." She slowly shook her head. "It can't be... you're in jail."

With a smug smile on his lips, Smitty said, "Oh, I can assure you it is."

Abbi watched in horror as he touched his jaw and worked an edge loose then pulled it upward. Dread washed over her as inch by inch the lifting of a silicon mask revealed the face of Raven.

He held out his hand once again. "Abbi?" When she didn't move quick enough to his liking, he pointed his pistol at Kim's head. "Now. Shall we?"

A wave of dizzying heat hit Abbi full force. Taking a deep calming breath, she slowly nodded placing her hand in his.

"You bastard!" Gwendolyn spat out. "It was you! You're the client Sheriff Martin was talking about. You're the man in charge. It was never him. You never intended on paying me for organizing the takedown of that plane!"

Raven spun around; his gun leveled at Gwendolyn's chest. "You're right. I never did have any intention. Do you think I could honestly pay you on the agreed upon amount?" He threw his head back and cackled. Raven looked at Abbi accusingly. "I would have if Ben never got the part in your movie. But that's okay, I'll take care of him later."

The bile rose in her throat as the pain in her stomach increased. Placing her hand on her belly she desperately tried to swallow it down, but it was no use. The projectile vomit hit Raven squarely in the face, momentarily blinding him.

Kim kicked out as Raven took a step back. He landed flat on his back, gagging, and wiping frantically at his face. With pure rage he jumped up and raised his gun, pointing it squarely at Abbi's chest.

"Not so fast asshole," Dean yelled. Slowly he entered the kitchen from the hallway, aiming his gun at Raven.

Tim was next, holding his gun on Gwendolyn.

"Raven you need to put that gun down right now!" Dean ordered him.

Never lowering his arm, Raven glanced at Dean and Tim while wiping his face on his sleeve. He dropped his gaze to Abbi and sneered. "Well how do you like that Abbi? Your man is nowhere in sight. Doesn't even have the *guts* to come and save you," he yelled, as his hand started to shake. To the room at large he said, "I'll tell you what I'm going to do. I'm going to shoot her and then... you two will shoot me. You see it's the perfect plan." He turned desperate eyes to Abbi. Insanely he whispered, "We'll always be together this way Abbi."

"Like hell you will." The ominous voice came from the darkened hall.

Raven spun towards it. Fear replaced the maniacal expression on his face as he saw an axe making it's spiraling way towards him. Shock registered in his eyes as the head buried itself deep in his chest. The last thing he saw before hitting the floor was a dark look on Ben's face.

Dean hobbled over to Mark and reached down to check for a pulse.

"He's breathing," he called out as sirens could be heard wailing in the distance.

Ben rushed to Abbi's side, catching her just before she hit the floor.

"Love are you okay?" His worried eyes searched her face.

She gripped his shirt as a wave of dizziness hit her again. She panted. "Yeah. "I'm just having a lot of cramping."

Ava stalked over to Gwendolyn, pulled back her arm and sucker punched her in the side of the face. The woman fell to the floor like a ton of bricks. "You ever kick my mother again I'll cut you."

"She kicked you?" Ben looked down at Abbi's ashen face. "Where?"

Kim looked at him, a grave expression on her face while she scrambled off the floor. "Her stomach. I'll call Doc."

Ben pulled a chair away from the table and dragged it to her side. "Come on, let's get you off the floor."

Once she was firmly sitting, Ben looked over to where Tim was. He was still holding his gun on Gwendolyn. Dean was sitting on the floor next to Mark, who was conscious now, pressing a towel against the gash on his head.

Ben was seething mad. Without thinking he walked up to Gwendolyn and wrapped his hands around her neck.

She grappled at his hands as they squeezed tighter. Her eyes protruding out of their sockets.

"Sonofabitch Ben!" Tim dropped his gun to the floor with a clatter as he tried pulling Ben off Gwendolyn. "Ava, give me a hand!" He shouted.

Ava jumped on Ben's back, pummeling it futilely. Abbi saw what he was doing. Despite wanting to do the same thing to the woman, she couldn't let him have that on his conscience too. Raven's death would be bad enough.

"Your baby needs its father, Ben."

Ben turned at the sound of her voice. Tears filled his eyes when he saw her arms wrapped around her middle. He dropped his hands and went to her. Sinking to his knees, he wrapped his arms around her, and softly placed his lips against her belly. Abbi ran her hands through his hair as she bent forward, she laid her head against his back. "And so, do I." Softly she cried against him. The pain once again wracked her body as her tears soaked his shirt.

Abbi couldn't hear what he was whispering against her stomach, but she knew his pain.

Please God... Don't let me lose them both...

Chapter 27

"Something didn't feel right back on the farm," Ben said, feeling the reassuring squeeze of Abbi's hand in his. He glanced at her. She was sitting beside him, silently conveying to him her love, giving him the strength to continue.

With everything that had happened since that fateful day; three days ago, when Raven decided to hold his family hostage, this was the first chance the police had of hearing his side of what happened. Cops, detectives, and agents from both sides of the border, were there to listen and gather information from all parties involved. They held Ben's fate in their hands.

He was thankful for Dave aka Dean. Despite the man's arrogant ways, he'd turned out to be a stand-up man. He'd insisted helping Tim to convince their fellow officers to hold off on questioning Ben, until Abbi and he found out if their baby was thriving.

Gently squeezing her hand back, he looked at the men in blue gathered around their dining room table.

"When did you discover there was something off?" A detective asked, his pen hovering over a notebook.

"I can't pinpoint when, just an overall feeling of foreboding." Ben thought a moment. Leaning forward, he said, "I think the fact that Smitty and Gwendolyn seemed to really know each other aside from the farm." Ben looked at Dave. "Just the way they talked about the plane crash, you know? Saying how lucky I was they were so close by." He frowned. "Plus, she took her mask off in front of him as if it were an everyday thing. I didn't realize until the other day that she really didn't know who he was either."

"And you didn't put the puzzle together until when?" The detective hedged.

"I had my suspicions. But it was when Raven shot him." Ben jerked his head to the man on his right, one that he now considered a friend. "Dean...er... Dave, had mentioned about the plane crash and used my stage name. That's when it occurred to me through the whole ordeal that only Raven, and Gwendolyn called me by my given name. To be honest. I thought Dave was somehow in on it."

"Well thanks for the vote of confidence there, bud." Dave shot him a sly smile.

An FBI agent cleared his throat. "With all due respect, Dave, you are a bit of an asshole."

The chief investigator stifled his chuckling with a cough. "I, ah think that pretty much clears up any unanswered questions." He paused. Looking directly at Ben, he said, "This is against protocol in situations like this. But due to your status and everything that has happened in the last few months I think we can come to a decision in what direction we will take. If you and Abbi will excuse us for a moment, we will let you know shortly."

Ben saw the look on Abbi's face as they left the room in silence. She was terrified. He guided her into the living room where everyone was waiting. Ava rushed over to them as they entered the room and tearfully hugged Ben. "I'm so sorry you're having to deal with this," she muttered. Pulling away, she hugged Abbi. "Mom. It's all going to work out."

"I know baby girl." Abbi hugged her back tightly, tears streaming down her eyes.

It has to work out.... She couldn't even begin to think what life would be like with Ben in a jail cell serving time for the death of Raven.

"So, now what?" Mark asked, scratching his head. He was currently sporting a bandage wrapped around it and was lucky that he only had a dozen stitches and a concussion.

Ben took a deep breath. "We wait."

Making his way to the window, he watched as big fluffy snowflakes made their way softly to the ground.

He wondered if the police did decide to arrest him, how long would it be before he could look out this window again. To look into Abbi's eyes again.

Days, months, years...?

His worried thoughts were interrupted with a car pulling in the driveway, followed by another... Abbi's SUV. Luke and Lane had arrived. He watched as his parents exited the first car followed by her sons and another man he'd never met before.

Ben turned to look at Abbi. She was sitting near him, in the chair by the fireplace. Looking forlorn. He gently touched her shoulder. "Love? Get the door, will you?"

He saw the instant puzzlement cross her lovely face. Grinning, he took her hand in his. "Trust me."

Together they walked to the door. She opened it and squealed at the sight of everyone standing there. Holding her arms wide, she embraced both her sons, as Ben's parents did the same to him.

A cough had everyone looking at the man that stood there alone.

Abbi frowned. *Why does he look so familiar...?*

"Oh, my goodness!!!" Abbi cried in delight. Holding her hands out to him, she welcomed him with a big hug.

"Abbi it's so good to see you again!" He laughed as he held her at arm's length. "I see you're going to have a little one." He beamed, looking down at the slight swell of her belly. "When are you due?"

"Yes!" She let him go and put an arm around Ben and smiled. "Mid May is when I'm due." Pointing over her shoulder, she said, "Um...will you excuse me for a moment?"

At his nod, she rushed to the living room, she had some quick explaining to do. "Hey Mark. How are you feeling?"

"Not too bad sweets." He gave her a sideways look. "Why do you ask?" She sat beside him and began talking in hushed tones.

"Like I said, I'm sorry, I completely forgot I'd asked Lane to bring him up when they came for Christmas. He was all alone though, and he did help me..."

Mark waved a hand at her. "I get it, I get it!" Leaning back against the couch, he rubbed the stubble on his chin, looking at her. "So, he knew me... but not Ben?"

Abbi nodded her head vigorously, grinning. "That's what he said."

She watched as he took a deep lungful of air. As proud as a peacock he said, "Well, what're you waiting for?" He grinned. "Bring him in."

Smiling, Abbi left his side and returned to the foyer, where only the man stood. "Where did everyone go? Never mind.

Come with me." She grabbed his arm and hurriedly steered him to the living room where Mark stood waiting.

"Mark, I'd like you to meet the cab driver who took me to the airport that night. Leo..." She looked to him realizing she had no idea what his last name was.

"Markell." He supplied standing there with his hat in his hand, grinning.

"Leo my man! What a coincidence, we have the same name. Mark, Markell... yeah. You know what I mean." Mark came forward with his hand outstretched. Chuckling, he said, "So, I hear you didn't know who Ben was?"

Abbi watched as Mark turned on the charm offering Leo a seat. She grinned knowing that she'd had a hand in making at least one person's wish come true.

The smile on her face stayed as she felt Ben come up behind her. Putting his arms around her, he laid his hands on her stomach. Softly he laid his lips against her neck. "Love, they are calling me back in the room now." Her smile faltered as she swallowed the lump that sprang to her throat and silently nodded. Turning within his embrace, she looked up and gazed into his eyes. Laying her hand on his cheek, she whispered, "I love you so much. Whatever happens I'll wait for you."

He laid his forehead against hers and covered her hand with his. "I love you too, sweet one." He softly kissed her on the lips, memorizing the feel of her mouth beneath his, clinging to her sweet taste. Wishing that he could stay in this moment forever.

From behind Ben, they heard Tim clear his throat. "Ben. They need to get on with this, the snow is picking up and they all have to get back to the city before the storm sets in."

Nodding, Ben backed away. Holding onto Abbi's hand he turned and followed Tim into the dining room. Pulling a chair out for her to sit he took the one next to her and sat down.

"Ben." The lead investigator began. "After careful consideration of the evidence at hand and all that has transpired in the past few months it is our opinion that charges against you in the death of Raven Black will..." The man stopped and looked at his fellow agents and officers. All nodded as one. The chief nodded back.

Abbi looked down to where her and Ben's hands were clasped in her lap.

Please God don't let them take him away from me, she silently pleaded as she squeezed his hand tight. So tight, his fingers were turning white from lack of blood flow.

Ben knew by the grip Abbi had on his hand that she would have a meltdown if the decision wasn't favorable. Hell, he was on the verge of one himself. Reaching over, he gently lifted her chin. Searching her eyes, he silently conveyed to her how much he loved her with just one look.

Clearing his throat for attention, the lead investigator continued. "Given the fact that you have two police officers to back your statement, we all believe the death of Raven Black was in self-defense and that you were protecting your family."

A cheer went up from the back of the room. Ben and Abbi turned as one, to look at their family and friends standing there.

Ben nodded his thanks at Tim, who nodded in return. He then looked at Dave who shot him a quick wink. Smiling, he turned back around to face the men before him.

"Not so fast." Banging the table for order as if he were a judge beating his gavel, the investigator continued when all fell silent.

"You possibly will need to go to court. Considering what Raven Black has done to you and Abbi in the past, I'll be talking to the crown attorney."

"As for the attack on Gwendolyn Pearce. It is felt by all of us that your actions were justified. Given the fact of everything she had done to both you and Abbi and that of your unborn child. And yes, even your dog. She, however, will face the consequences of her actions and will be charged for all offenses she has committed, which is quite lengthy. Charges against you, will not be filed for now at least not, that may change when I speak to the Crown. Stay in the country and you're free to do whatever you please." The investigator stood up, looked at his fellow officers and said "Let's get out of here. We have a long trip home."

IT HAD BEEN A WEEK since the investigators had come and gone. The house was silent as Ben and Abbi laid in each other's arms. Their house guests had long since retired to their rooms, all caught up in the excitement of Christmas Eve.

She snuggled up to him, laying her head on his chest she listened to the steady beat of his heart as he absently drew his fingers over her bare skin.

He was watching the news on the TV. The reporter came on with breaking headline news. Abbi sat up, watching, as scenes from the plane crash played across the screen; it felt like yesterday when Ava had burst through the door telling her the news. Ben sat up beside her, putting his arm around her, he pulled her close to his side.

"It has been confirmed that Ben Everett leading actor of the Jasper Killings and soon to be released movie, Stoned River has been found alive and well." The male announcer said.

"Took them long enough." Ben snickered, looking at Abbi.

She covered his mouth with her hand and left it there. "Shush."

"Coincidentally, it was found that the actor's plane had been purposely shot down. Investigators linked it to Raven Black, the same actor, who not more than a few months ago made headline news by getting bail" The announcer looked to his co-anchor *"Get this... after an attempted murder on Ben Everett. Raven Black was found dead by a self-inflicted gunshot wound in his home."*

Abbi turned to Ben and sent him a dumbfounded look. "Wha—"

He placed his finger on her lips, hushing her this time.

"Wow! What a crazy mixed-up world we live in." The female announcer added.

"That's not even the half of it. Ben Everett the most sought-after actor in Hollywood just announced his retirement...."

Ben clicked the remote to turn the TV off, as he did, he laid a soft kiss in the palm of Abbi's hand, the one that still covered his mouth. He laid back and pulled her on top of him.

She gestured to the TV. "What was that all about?"

"I forgot to mention to you that Simon Smith, you remember the lead investigator...?" He looked at her with his brows raised. At her nod, he continued. "Yeah. Anyway, he called earlier this morning and told me he'd talked to the Crown. They are not going forward with any charges against me and there will be no court proceedings. That's the reason for the story of Raven '*shooting himself*.'"

He looked in her eyes, watching and waiting for a reaction. When there wasn't one, he reached out and brushed the hair out of her eyes. "What're you thinking love?"

She sighed. "I'm thinking... That I am the luckiest woman in the world right about now." She smiled looking down at him.

He raised a brow. A quick devilish smile flitted on his lips. "Oh yeah?"

"Mhm. I got my Christmas wish." She smiled, as she kissed his chest. Feeling his heartbeat quicken at her touch, she slowly made her way up to his lips. She felt so utterly moved by him as she clung to his mouth.

When he reached up and grabbed her by the arms, she let out a squeal of laughter as he flipped her onto her back.

They both grinned at one another as he sat back and straddled her legs.

Abbi looked at him. Watched as his face took on a serious note.

"What is it?" She asked, her smile wavering.

"Back there, on the farm. I thought I would never see you again. If anything had happened to me, I'd have died never knowing that I was going to be a father... I thank God every day for bringing you into my life Abbi Petersen."

"Ben." She sat up, tears stinging her eyes. Gazing deeply into his, she saw the love shine there for her.

"Abbi. You are the love of my life; the mother of my child and I can't wait for the day that you become my wife." He took her face in his hands. Kissing her with a fiery hunger as he laid her back on the bed.

She sighed contentedly. When he nuzzled her neck, her insides turned to mush, and then she giggled uncontrollably when he growled next to her ear.

"Woman you drive me insane."

She silently thanked God and the Universe for bringing this man home to her. All that she'd wanted for Christmas, and for the rest of her days was right there in her arms.

The End

I hope you enjoyed Ben and Abbi's story again. I love reviews so please feel free to leave one.

Now read on for a look into Ava and Mark's story,

Heaven in the Moonlight

Prologue

"WHAT DO YOU MEAN, I can't get a discount?!" The woman all but screamed across the counter into the young woman's face.

Ava stood, staring at the lady in shock. The last customer of the day and of course she just had to start yelling. Instead of yelling back, Ava mentally cursed out her Aunt Kim. She would need to remember to thank her for sending such a tyrant to her shop.

She inhaled a slow calming breath and counted to ten.

"Ma'am. I'm sorry, but company policy does not allow for a discount on our already discounted promotional packages. Not to mention you did get $50.00 off for the friends and family discount." Ava replied in what she hoped was her sweetest tone.

The melodious tune from the door opening, announced that a new customer had just walked in as the woman continued her rantings.

"I demand to speak to the owner." The woman puffed out her cheeks, making her look like a blowfish that was about to pop.

"Cool your jets there, Claudia." Kim piped up as she sauntered in. Laughing, she asked, "What's got your knickers in a twist now?" She propped her arms on the counter and leaned forward, looking at the woman.

"This..." Claudia looked at Ava with distaste. "...girl refused to get the owner after I had a valid complaint!"

Ava made a small cry of protest at the lie the woman just told.

"Is that so?" Kim arched a brow as she glanced at Ava. She directed her attention back to the crotchety woman. "And what is it you need to speak to the owner about?" Kim couldn't help grinning, knowing that Claudia was about to be in for a rude awakening.

Not that Kim disliked Claudia. She didn't really know her all that well. Aside of her being a patient at the doctor's office where Kim worked as a nurse. A patient that claimed she was in 'desperate need of some pampering' or so Claudia declared to her just last week. The woman did rub people the wrong way with her demanding attitude. Old money ran deep in that family and Kim supposed it was from ordering all her servants around.

"I simply asked for a discount on the package I purchased. $150 is a little steep in my opinion for the services that were rendered." She sniffed.

Apparently, Claudia was cheap too. Kim snorted. She knew there wasn't a finer spa in the city than Ava's.

That remark had Ava seething. Considering it was already half price, the woman was delusional if she thought she was getting it any cheaper.

"Here, let me see the bill." Kim snatched the paper off the counter and noted the smug smile on Claudia's face. She scanned the page and smacked it back down, pointing at it. She looked at Claudia and said, "Seeing how you were already talking to the owner, who happens to be my niece, she can fix this right now."

"Ava, here is your mistake. You gave her a discount for the friends and family... which she is neither." Kim smiled sweetly at Claudia as she walked around the counter to stand beside Ava.

Together, they watched as Claudia turned every colour of the rainbow as she dug in her purse for her wallet. "I've never been treated with such disrespect in my life!" Claudia spat, tossing her credit card on the bill.

"Yeah. Well, that's your prob—"

A sharp elbow to her ribs had Kim shutting up. Ava tossed her a dark look as she processed the payment and handed the woman her card back.

Snatching it from Ava, Claudia spun on her heel then stopped. She looked turned to look back and said, "I will be sure to tell all my friends about this! And Kim, you can be assured I'll be telling Dr. Wellington about your conduct!"

Kim made a face at Claudia's back, mocking her as she exited the building.

"I could have handled that Aunt Kim. What if she tells Dr. Wellington, what will you do?" Ava knew her aunt was already on thin ice with her boss. The thought of all the customers she'd likely lose once word got around, caused Ava's brow to knit with worry as she went to lock the door.

"Oh, I know you could. And I never thought of that to be honest. I just wanted to put that woman in her place once and for all. She treats the world like shit but expects to be treated like she is the Queen of England or something." Kim stifled a yawn. "So where are we going for dinner, I'm starving."

"I thought we would try that new place over on Sunnyside, if that's all right with you?" Ava said, turning the sign in the window to close.

"Sounds good to me."

"Okay, can you give Luke a call? He and Lane are going to meet us wherever we decided on. I just need to do my till and then we can go." Ava pulled the drawer out of the cash register, listening with half an ear, she heard Kim chatting away as she headed to her office.

"OOH THIS IS NICE." Kim looked around in awe as she took her seat. Her eyes settled on the gleaming hardwood of the massive staircase that sat in the centre of the dining area of the Edge of the Sea restaurant.

Lane nodded. Grabbing a chair, he pulled it out and sat. "Yeah, it's surprising what they can do to an old riverboat. Just wait till we leave the dock."

Kim's eyes zeroed in on Lane's face. "Wait." Giggling nervously, she gripped his arm like a vise. With a hurried hiss, she asked, "What did you say?" She was glancing around furtively, looking for the closest exit when they felt the smooth rocking of the ship slip forward.

"Oh, hell no. I can't do this." Kim shook her head vehemently while she grabbed her purse and stood up. "Let's go."

Lane pried her hand off his arm and looked up at her. "Aunt Kim it will be fine, it just goes up the river and back. I promise, you'll forget you're on a boat once the food comes."

Ava tugged on Kim's arm and urging her aunt to sit down, once she flopped onto her chair, Ava looked at her brother. "I thought Luke was coming too?"

The waiter's arrival momentarily stopped their conversations. With menus tucked under his arm and a tray full of ice water balanced on the other, he somehow managed to sit a coffee pot on the table without it all toppling over.

"Hey guys." He grinned as handed them each a menu. "I'm Brian and I'll be your gopher tonight. Can I get you folks some drinks before you order?"

Ava smiled. "Water is fine for me."

Kim was fighting the sting of bile that rose in the back her throat. "Do you have a Gravol margarita by chance?"

The Brian stared at her blankly.

She shook her head. "No? ... water it is." She picked up a glass and chugged half of it before setting it back on the table. A loud burp escaped past her lips.

Ava noticed Brian masked his outburst of laughter pretty quick by faking a cough.

Waving a hand in front of her face, Kim said, "Whoa, s'cuse me, no idea where that came from."

She was oblivious to the stares and snickers from the other patrons, but Lane wasn't. Shielding his face with his hand, he flipped a cup over that was sitting on the table. "Coffee is good enough for me, thanks." He watched as the waiter skillfully poured the piping hot liquid.

"I'll give you a few minutes to decide," Brian said, as he made a quick exit.

Lane glanced at his watch. "Ah... Luke is supposed to be here." He scanned the room for his twin, then jerked his head towards the bar. "There he is."

All eyes turned to look. There, stood Luke talking to a striking black-haired beauty. Luke saw them the same instant. Tugging on the woman's hand, they made their way towards the table.

Kim snorted, as she fished an ice cube out of her glass. "Who is that? The new flavour of the week?"

"Kim!" Ava hissed. "What is *wrong* with you?"

"What?! I know you're thinking the same thing. Don't deny it missy." She popped the ice cube in her mouth and grinned as the couple sat down.

"Hey guys." Luke looked around the table. "I want you to meet Cassie my girlfriend. Cassie, this is my sister Ava, Aunt Kim and you know Lane."

"Nice to meet you." Ava smiled while Kim kept silent grinning like a fool.

The waiter came back just then and took their order, assuring them the wait wouldn't be too long.

Ava pushed her glass out of the way and laid her arms on the table, leaning forward she looked at Luke. "So. How long have you two been dating?"

Kim giggled. "Oh about—"

Ava shot her aunt a glare. Knowing she was about to say something totally inappropriate, she said, "Aunt Kim, eat more ice." She placed another glass in front of Kim with a thud.

"What?!" Kim said accusingly.

"You know what!" Ava pointed to the glass. "Eat. The. Ice!"

Touching a finger to her temple, Ava said, "Now, where were we? Oh right, how long have you two been dating?"

Cassie looked from Ava to Kim, then Luke. "Is your aunt alright?" She turned her attention back to Ava. "You know I heard that when people need to eat ice it's because they are lacking something. It's called pica... I think. Kim did you eat paint chips or feces as a child?"

"Sweet baby Jesus. Now look at what you did Ava! The girl thinks I'm a shit eater."

Lane burst out laughing at the same moment Ava kicked Kim under the table, imploring her with her eyes to be nice.

Eyes flashing, Kim didn't say a word. Instead, she stuck her fingers into the water and fished out a nice square cube. Popping it in her mouth she sent a sarcastic smile at her niece. Ava knew her better than anyone at the table.

"Ah, we have been together for a week. I'm bringing her to meet Mom when we go up for May 24," Luke said, gazing into Cassie's eyes.

Kim whipped her head around to look at Luke. *Bring her to meet Abbi... is he nuts?*

All the sudden, she could feel her eyes bug out of her head... the ice cube went down the wrong hole. Clutching her throat all she could think about was the regret of not leaving the restaurant. She should have swum to shore.

"Aunt Kim are you alright?" Ava cried in alarm. Feeling guilty that she told her to eat the ice in the first place, Ava stood and smacked Kim on the back.

"Jesus Ava, you're going to break her ribs. Here Aunt Kim, take a sip." Lane handed her his coffee cup.

Kim took a gulp of the scalding coffee. It melted the ice cube alright, because it made a searing path down to the pit of her stomach. "Thanks," she gasped as she set the cup on the table, she wiped the tears that sprang to the corners of her eyes on her sleeve.

Concern was etched on Ava's face. "Are you okay?"

"Yeah. I'm good."

"Good." Ava sat back in her chair. "Okay. So, I wanted to know from you two how do we convince mom to move back home?" she asked, looking at her brothers.

She missed their mother more than they did. Having done everything with her, it was a hard pill to swallow, when she upped and moved to Pearl Lake. Ava didn't blame her. After her mom's book hit the number one on the New York Times best sellers list, some crazed fan was after her. Abbi pulled up stakes and was gone in the blink of an eye.

"Oh, would you look at that!" Cassie said, all eyes turned to see the waiter carrying a large tray with their food.

"Ava, you can't, that's how. Your mom is finally happy. You can't expect her to move back here. She's made a home there." Kim reasoned. With a fear of tossing her cookies, she took her plate from the waiter.

"But she's alone, and since the break-in I worry about her constantly." Ava sighed.

"Well, I don't think she's alone. Not anymore." Lane leaned back as the waiter placed a heaping plate of food in front of him.

Luke smiled. "What do you mean she's not anymore?"

"When I called and to tell her we would be up Thursday, she said she was going to invite a friend over." Lane shrugged his shoulders. "Said his name was Ben."

"Ben? Ben, who?" Kim asked, munching on a fry.

"She didn't say. Nor did she say what kind of friend."

Ava thoughts turned to the worst scenario. In her mind, she could picture exactly what he looked like. The type that was only after one thing. Money. She pushed her food around with her fork. "Why don't we surprise her and go up early. Beat the traffic?" She was ready to leave this second, the sooner the better as far as she was concerned. She wanted to see what this friend of her mother's was really like. "Well?" she asked, impatiently.

"How soon were you thinking?" Luke asked, checking his phone to see if he had any meetings for the rest of the week.

"Now."

"Are you crazy Ava?" Lane bit out. "We can't just leave now."

"Why not? All of us have the luxury of just picking up and leaving without the worry of being fired. And besides, how long has it been since we've seen mom? Christmas, that's how long. Don't you think that's been long enough?" Ava asked.

"She does have a point." Kim nodded vigorously.

Lane looked at Luke, who then looked at Cassie then back to Luke. Glancing at his sister, he threw his hands in the air. "Sure, why not?"

"Yes!" Ava squealed. Jumping up, she ran around the table to hug her brothers.

"Ahem." Kim cleared her throat.

All sets of eyes turned to Kim. "What about you Kim, you have any plans for the next week or so?" Luke asked.

"I can't say that I do, I'm off for a month." Her thoughts turned to Claudia and the display she had caused in Ava's shop. She smoothed a hand over her hair and mumbled, "Um, likely indefinitely."

"Then it's settled. Let's get out of here." Ava headed back to her chair to collect her belongings; she grabbed her cellphone to check the time. Tossing three, hundred-dollar bills on the table, she said, "We can all meet at our place if you like."

At her brother's nod, she headed towards the exit. "Come on Aunt Kim, let's go home and pack."

You can find their story by clicking the link or cover below!
<u>Heaven in the Moonlight.</u>[1]

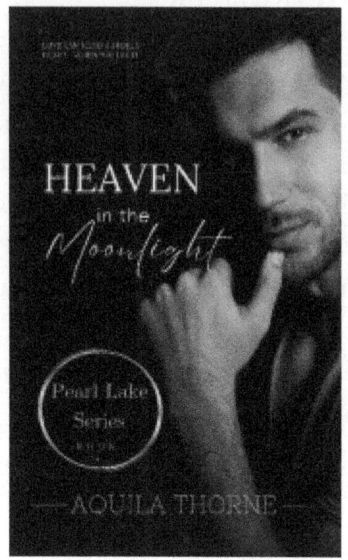

[2]

1. https://books2read.com/ATHeavenintheMoonlight

2. https://books2read.com/ATHeavenintheMoonlight

Did you love *Moonlit Road*? Then you should read *Heaven in the Moonlight*[3] by Aquila Thorne!

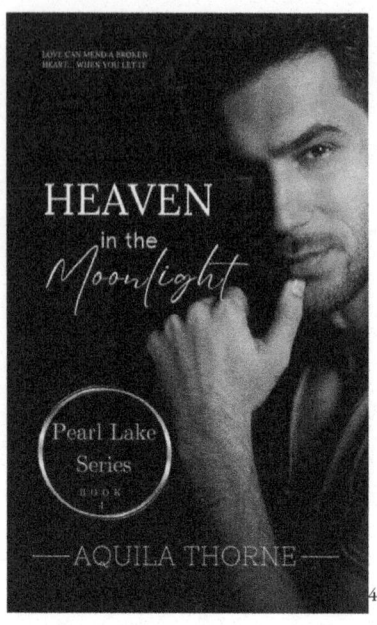

[4]

Can love mend a broken heart, it will when you find the 'one'...

Wanting to be near her mom Abbi, Ava Petersen sold her spa in her hometown and moved to Pearl Lake; but that wasn't the only reason she did. She needed a new place to escape from her wounded past and moving in with her aunt Kim and new friend, actor Mark Donovan, is the perfect plan. Except, he's her celebrity crush.

---

3. https://books2read.com/u/mdd1ZX

4. https://books2read.com/u/mdd1ZX

Mark has been kicking himself ever since he sold his property on the shores of the picturesque village to his best friend, Ben. So, after Ben and Abbi move in together. Mark does the next best thing and rents her house next door. Bonus points: Ava moves in too. The problem is, he's fallen for her and hard.

When he finally gets the nerve to tell her how he feels, in walks Ash Davenport. A Texan that has his eyes set on Ava.

Feeling like he's been sucker-punched in the gut, Mark recruits Kim to put their amateur sleuth skills to work and to find out the truth about the newcomer. But they didn't bargain on finding the makings of a nightmare. It leaves them wondering...Will anyone in Pearl Lake live to see another day?

Hey everyone, it's Ava. I just wanted to mention that there are triggers of abuse in this book. Nothing too serious but enough that some people could relate to more than others. There is also plenty of laughs, and a touch of suspense too. Just wanted to let you know before you dug into my story~ Love, Ava xoxo

Made in the USA
Monee, IL
06 August 2023

40515536R00152